click here

click here

(to find out how i survived seventh grade)

a novel by denise vega

LITTLE, BROWN AND COMPANY
New York Boston

Little, Brown and Company

Time Warner Book Group
1271 Avenue of the Americas, New York, NY 10020
Visit our Web site at www.lb-teens.com

First Edition: April 2005

The characters and events portrayed in this book are fictitious. Any similarity to real persons, living or dead, is coincidental and not intended by the author.

Cover photography (lollipop image) © Lucky Pix.
Other photos courtesy of Getty Images.

Library of Congress Cataloging-in-Publication Data

Vega, Denise.
Click here : (to find out how I survived seventh grade) / by Denise Vega. — 1st ed.
p. cm.
Summary: Seventh-grader Erin Swift writes about her friends and classmates in her private blog, but when it accidentally gets posted on the school Intranet site, she learns some important lessons about friendship.
ISBN 0-316-98560-0
[1. Friendship — Fiction. 2. Interpersonal relations — Fiction.
3. Weblogs — Fiction. 4. Computers — Fiction. 5. Middle schools — Fiction.
6. Schools — Fiction.] I. Title.
PZ7.V4865Cl 2005
[Fic] — dc22 2004016164

10 9 8 7 6 5 4 3 2 1

Q-FF

Printed in the United States of America
Book design by Alison Impey.
The text was set in Life Roman and Trebuchet MS, and the display type is Badoni.

To Nancy Roach,

my seventh- and eighth-grade literature teacher and still my friend. For making me believe, at the age of twelve, that I was a writer.

ACKNOWLEDGMENTS

First novelists always tend to thank the entire world, and I'm no different, though I promise not to thank the shoe salesperson or the guy in the checkout line behind me.

First, big hugs to my family: my husband, Matt Perkins, and my kids, Zachary, Jesse Bernadette, and Rayanne Vega-Perkins. You rock. To my extended family and friends, who supported and continued to support my writing: my parents, John and Carol Vega; my brother, John Vega, and his wife, Eva Page Vega; my sisters, Michelle and her husband, Wayne Applehans, Cheryl VegaRyan and her husband, James Ryan, and Rebecca Vega; my mother-in-law, Elizabeth Perkins, and her late husband, Bill Perkins, and Bill Jr., Susie, and Sarah Perkins. To all my friends at St. Vincent de Paul School who picked up kids, watched kids, delivered kids, or stood kids on their heads when I needed a little extra writing time. I'm afraid to name you all lest I forget someone, but you know who you are.

Big non-Vegamite kudos to both of my critique groups, whose words of wisdom as they tore my work apart bit by bit and helped me put it back together again, made the manuscript immeasurably better. Here they are, in alphabetical order: Hilari Bell, Meridee Jones Cecil, Carol Crowley, Anna-Maria Crum, Julie Danneberg, Coleen DeGroff, Wick Downing, Amy Efaw, Vicki Ferguson, Claudia McAdam, Marjorie Blain Parker, Christine Liu Perkins, Julie Anne Peters, Shawn Shea, Bobbi Shupe, Caroline Stutson, Ann Sullivan, and Rick Winter.

Special thanks to Julie Anne Peters, who graciously opened the door to Little, Brown Books for Young Readers, and to those at Little, Brown who welcomed me inside: Megan Tingley, Jennifer Hunt, Sara Morling, Phoebe Sorkin, and Michael "I'm leaving to get a master's degree" Conathan. Thank you for your humor, support, and insights into the manuscript. I'm so glad I stepped through. And thanks to copyeditor Christine Cuccio, whose eagle eye saved me from embarrassment.

Many thanks to my agent, Wendy Schmalz, for agreeing to take a chance on a new author (and thanks to Julie Peters for introducing us). You're the best.

And finally, thank you to my friends at the Denver Public Library, especially at the Eugene Field Branch: Susan Gomez, DuRae Kubat, and Kathi Yuran. I can't thank you enough for tirelessly checking out my stacks of children's novels, lugging my reserves from the back, and always making me smile.

my life

My Life | Mug Shots | MBMS | Snickers

Erin's Website...Keep Out! (This Means YOU!)

This is the totally secret and private home page of ERIN PENELOPE SWIFT. I guess it's kind of like a fake web page, because most web pages are seen by lots of people on the Internet and mine will only be seen by me. But I don't care. If I want to be a webmaster when I grow up, I need to practice.

Besides, I need to talk about some things, and Jilly isn't always around to listen...and even when she is, she is not always the best listener, though I would never tell her that because she's my best friend and it might hurt her feelings.

Things You Should Know About Me

- I have big feet, which is great for basketball and soccer, bad for dancing. Luckily I play basketball and soccer, and no 1 has asked me to dance.

- Jillian Gail Hennessey is my best friend and has been since K. She's very pretty and friendly, and everyone likes her. Sometimes I can't believe she wants me for her friend.

- I have an older brother, Chris. Now that he's a sophomore in h.s. and can DRIVE, he treats me like I'm a pest. Chris wears stupid bright orange boxers with green frogs on them, checks his breath by breathing into his hand and smelling it, and tucks pictures of the girls he likes under a box on his dresser. Sometimes he takes 1 out and talks to it, like he's talking to the girl. He doesn't know I know.

Info About the Links 

My Life

will be stuff about me and my exciting life. This will be the blog or live journal part, with dates and stuff . . . not really live since no 1 else will read it, but whatever.

Mug Shots

will have pictures of the zillions of people in my life. Or if I don't make any new friends, it will just be me and Jilly.

MBMS

will be stuff about Molly Brown Middle School, my new prison, that I think is worth sharing.

Snickers

will be for when I get tired of clicking and just want to have a Snickers.

Ok, TTFN.

KEEP OUT!

Don't like this website? 2 bad!

The webmaster does NOT want to hear from you.

The Ped Stops Here!

chapter 1

Alphabet Day

D-Day.

Or should I say E-Day, as in Envelope Day. Jilly and I stood on her front porch, fighting for the small amount of shade from the maple planted several feet from the house. The air was still and hot, and we fanned ourselves in quick bursts with the identical envelopes we clutched in our hands. In these envelopes were our futures. Molly Brown Middle School divided each seventh- and eighth-grade class into three "tracks" of about 150 kids. So rather than feeling like a small fish in a 450-student pond, we'd feel like a small fish in a 150-student pond, going to all our classes with a mix of these 150 kids.

We were about to find out if we'd be swimming in the same pond.

"Ready?" Jilly asked.

My heart bounced up and down in my chest. "I'm nervous," I said. "What if we're not on the same track?"

"Don't jinx it, Erin." Jilly stuck her finger in one corner of her envelope, ready to rip.

"One, two, three!"

We tore open the envelopes. "C," Jilly said at the same time that I said, "A."

"Ahhhhh," I wailed. "I jinxed it."

"This is terrible," Jilly said, jumping off the porch and sinking into the grass. "Are you sure you read yours right?"

A and C don't exactly look the same, but I held my letter out to her anyway.

"A," she muttered. "This is the worst."

I flopped down next to her. It was worse than the worst. It was a disaster. We'd only been separated once in elementary school. We'd always been in class together. Always.

"I can't walk to classes by myself," Jilly said.

"I know."

"Oh, God," Jilly said, sitting up. "I can't go into the cafeteria by myself."

The cafeteria, aka the Humiliation Station. I hadn't even thought about that. All those eyes turning to stare as I walked in, seeing right away that I was BY MYSELF, which meant no one to whisper secrets to or laugh with as we looked for a table, which meant no way to look like I fit in, which meant LOSER.

I wrapped my arms around my knees, in spite of the heat. "What are we going to do?"

Jilly frowned. "I need to think about this." She stroked her legs, which were freshly shaved and unmarked. I admired that. I always had at least one cut and usually missed a whole area near my ankle so that I had a little clump of fur that I didn't notice until I was nowhere near a razor. But she always got every spot so her legs were smooth and unblemished.

Jilly slapped the grass on either side of her and jumped to her feet. "Let's go shopping."

"How can you think of shopping at a time like this?"

"It's just the thing to take our minds off of it," Jilly said. "The ideas will come if we're not thinking about it."

I hated to shop. Especially for clothes, which Jilly loved to do. Comfort before style. That was my motto. But I had to admit I wanted to look good for seventh grade. I was practically a teenager and almost-teens needed to have style and flare, even if they had feet the size of a small whaling ship. And Jilly was the queen of style and flare. If it wasn't for her, I'd look like a moron.

"I've got just the thing for you," Jilly said, as if reading my mind. "It'll knock the socks off the MBMS boys."

"I don't want to knock their socks off," I said. "What if their feet stink?"

Jilly laughed. "Well, then, let's knock their hats off. Boys always wear hats."

We both giggled. But then I felt a little twinge in my belly. Did I really want to knock socks, hats, or any other clothing off a boy's body? That would make them notice me, which would immediately reveal my boy/girl loser status.

"So, shopping?" Jilly's face lit up, as if she was asking me to go to Web Design World (the ultimate web design conference) or a WNBA game, not just the boring mall.

"Sure," I said reluctantly.

"I saw these really cute jeans at PacSun," Jilly said.

"All they have are low-waist jeans," I said. "We're not allowed to show our belly button at Molly Brown."

"That's what shirts are for, Erin," Jilly said. "I put jeans and a cool T-shirt on hold for you."

I made a face.

"What?" Jilly asked. "It's jeans and a T-shirt. That's what you like to wear, right?"

I nodded. But not those kind of jeans. I liked regular jeans, not the ones that sat low on my nonexistent hips. And why did she have to put them on hold as if it were a done deal?

"So, what's the problem?"

"Well, I'd kind of like to try them on first."

Jilly laughed. "Duh. I just put them on hold so they'd be there if we wanted them."

Of course. It wasn't like I had to get the outfit if I didn't want it. "Thanks."

• • •

After we'd bought the PacSun outfit, Jilly grabbed my arm and squeezed. "You're going to look so cute in that."

I had to admit I liked what I'd seen in the dressing-room mirror. My hips were still nonexistent, but the jeans weren't too low and they made it seem like there was a little curve there. Last time Jilly had me try on some that, if I bent too far over, made my butt crack show. I'd prefer not to share my crack with the rest of the world, thank you very much.

"If you wore bikini underwear, that wouldn't be a problem," she had told me.

"Bikini underwear feels like it's going to fall off," I said. And a thong was like purposely giving yourself a wedgie all day long. Why would you do that? I couldn't believe some girls wore them. Personally, I liked my underwear to have some substance. Especially because I played sports and didn't want to worry about butt cracks or wedgies during a layup.

"I'll be over to pick out your clothes on Sunday," Jilly said as we left the store.

I gave her the thumbs-up. She came over every Sunday, picked my outfits for the week, and made a list for me. It was great because I always looked good, even though sometimes I felt like an idiot for not being able to do it myself.

As we headed down the mall, Jilly stopped. "Oh, my God! Duh." She turned to me. "You'll switch tracks. I can't believe I didn't think of it before." She snapped her fingers the way she always does when she gets an idea. "Have your mom call the school in the morning and get you on C Track."

"Okay," I said. I kind of wanted to be on A Track because it was closer to the computer lab, a point I'd noticed when we visited the school last year. But that was okay.

"Good," Jilly said. She sighed as we headed to the main entrance where we were meeting her mother. "I can't imagine going through seventh grade without you."

I smiled. "Me neither."

• • •

ETM (Evil Torture Mom) refused to call the school. "They don't allow switching unless there are special circumstances," she said. "The policy hasn't changed since Chris went there."

"This is special," I protested. "It's beyond special. It's catastrophic."

"It's all about balance," Mom said. "They carefully select the students for each track based on several factors."

"One switch is not going to change the balance, Mom." My insides sank all the way down to my heels, settling in somewhere around my calluses.

My mom shook her head, and I called in a report to Jilly.

"What if you find someone who would switch to A?" she said. Brilliant.

I headed for the desk in the kitchen, opening the drawer where we kept the school directory. I knew which kids from Jordan Elementary were going to MBMS. I explained the plan to my mom, who was chopping potatoes at the counter.

"Erin." Mom stopped chopping and looked at me. I didn't meet her eyes.

"After I find someone, you can call the school." Confidence surged through me with this new plan. "I don't know if I can promise I'll find a girl with big feet who likes basketball and computers, but I'll try."

I could feel Mom smile and knew her eyes were full of compassion. "Erin."

"Would you stop saying my name?" I held my finger in mid-dial and looked at her. "Even if I find someone, you're not going to call for a switch, are you?"

My mom sighed. "Even if I thought they'd go for it, I don't think I would. This is an opportunity for you to spread your wings, Erin."

I gripped the phone. "I don't have any wings, Mom."

"You don't have any other friends, either," Chris said. He had shuffled in just then, treading his usual path to the refrigerator.

"Shut up." I dropped the phone back in its cradle.

"Honey," my mom said, coming to stand beside me.

"You're so mean!" I said. "You could call right now and keep Jilly and me together, but you won't do it. I hate you!" I ran out of the room and up the stairs. Slamming the door behind me, I flung myself on the bed, burying my face in my arms.

A few minutes later there was a knock at my door.

"Erin?" Mom spoke softly, as if I might be sleeping. "Erin, can I come in?"

"No!" I shouted, even though I realized in that instant that I did want her to. I waited. If she asked again, I'd say yes.

After what seemed like hours but was probably just a few seconds, Mom spoke. "If you want to talk, I'll be in my office."

I snorted. I wasn't going to go to *her.* Besides, what was there to talk about? She had deliberately decided to ruin my life and there was nothing I could do about it.

"We'll figure something out," Jilly said when she called that night to find out what had happened. "We're best friends. They can't keep us apart."

"Right," I said. But inside I had a feeling they could.

Monday, August 19

Ok, so this is my 2nd blog entry. Hooray. I'm into lists, which you probably figured out from my very 1st entry...hmm. Who am I talking to? I guess it's that mysterious "Dear Diary" person. Anyway, I like lists, so whatever.

Things That Are Freaking Me Out

- I start at MBMS TOMORROW and Jilly can't go! She has strep! Mom didn't believe me when I said I thought I had strep, 2.
- The bus stop will have 8th graders. 8th graders scare me.
- Who's going to help me navigate the great halls of MBMS? Who's going to pick my seat (the chair, not my butt)?
- Jilly wants me to make a map of her classes. She wants 2 versions: the shortest route and a route that goes by the gym so she can check out the guys. Yikes!
- I have BIG FEET at a new school...possible tease opportunity. Everyone at Jordan Elem. knows my feet and has kind of forgotten about them...but the new kids who don't know me won't know my BIG FEET.
- I'm so scared and nervous I think I might throw up.

Why I Know My Family Has No Heart 

- My mom refused to let me switch tracks.
- My brother laughed and rolled his eyes at me...hello?...He practically threw up the day B4 his 1st day of high school.
- My parents have NO memory of what it's like to be 12.
- My parents both said, "You'll live." I will NOT live...and when the school calls and they have to come claim my body cuz I died of Freak Out, they'll be very, very sorry.

Things That Make Me Wonder 

- Why doesn't Jilly try to switch to my track?
- Why am I afraid to ask her to switch?
- Why do I have to ask questions like that?

Will Erin P. Swift survive MBMS? Stay tuned.

chapter 2

First Day Freakout

I sat in my seat, stomach in knots, praying to the barf gods that I wouldn't throw up. Especially on my new outfit.

The school bus lurched and moaned as it pulled away from my stop. Three unopened Snickers were tucked in my backpack, and I wondered if I'd ever feel like eating them.

Something sharp poked my thigh and I glanced down. The pin Jilly had given me for good luck stuck through my shorts. I wasn't wearing it because it had a rolling clasp that I could never seem to keep on. The pin was one of those dual drama masks — the smiling one for comedy, the frowning one for tragedy. Jilly was big into drama. I'd put tape over the tragedy face — only happy times for Erin P. Swift on her first day at Molly Brown Middle School.

My eyes shifted to the empty seat beside me and my stomach flipped again. How could I be sitting on a strange bus, going to a new school, all by myself? I told my mom I needed to stay with Jilly, but she practically laughed in my face, something that isn't a particularly good quality in a parent, in my opinion. Too bad no one asked my opinion. But I had to admit it felt good to talk to her the night before, even though I was still a little mad at her for not supporting OST (Operation Switch Tracks).

"I've never been separated from Jilly," I told her last night.

My mom opened her arms and I stepped in, not caring that almost-teens shouldn't hug their parents.

"It's going to be hard, Erin. I know that. You and Jilly have been inseparable." She stroked my hair, tucking it behind my ear the way I liked.

"Just thinking about walking into that humongous school and going right while Jilly goes left and not seeing her until the end of the day . . ." Tears stung my eyes. "Please let me stay home," I whispered.

My mom squeezed me tight in reply. "Maybe in a few days you can start looking at this as an adventure. New friends, new situations."

"I don't want anything new." I sniffled into her shirt. I wished we could stop time and all go back to Jordan Elementary where I knew everyone and what to do and how to act.

My mom pulled back gently and took my face in her hands. "You can do this, Erin."

I wished I could believe her.

I turned my eyes away from the bus window, staring at the head of the kid in front of me. He had one of those haircuts where the top half looked like it was cut around a bowl and the bottom part was shaved. Red bumps swelled where the razor had gotten too close near the nape of his neck. Ugh. I was examining somebody's scalp at close range. What was wrong with me?

As kids got on, the seat next to me stayed empty. Part of me wondered why — I'd put on extra deodorant this morning — and part of me was glad. It was like people knew the spirit of Jilly was sitting there and were respecting it.

Smack. A rather large butt in faded jeans squashed Jilly's spirit, settling into the thin green cushion.

"Um," I murmured.

"What?" The boy narrowed his eyes, daring me to say something. "You can't save seats, you know. Against the rules."

"Whatever," I mumbled, not knowing if there was a rule or not. It didn't really matter, though, because I didn't have anyone to save it for anyway.

"Man, are those peds for real?" The boy stared at my feet.

I glared at him before looking down at my high tops. I'd been wearing Chuck Taylors since first grade. They were comfortable and light. And not only that, I could wear a size 8 men's Chuck, instead of a women's 10 sneaker. So I stuck with Chuck.

"Well, are they?" The boy's voice brought me back. I raised a Chuck. "I can step on your face and you can decide for yourself."

"Oooh," the boy murmured in mock fear, leaning toward me.

"Hey, Eddie! Don't kiss her! You'll get foot-and-mouth disease."

The boy — Eddie — looked down at my feet again and grimaced. "I'm out of here," he said, pushing up from the seat.

I sighed with relief, hardly believing I'd said what I'd said. I had no idea where it had come from but was glad it had. I tapped Jilly's pin lightly through my shorts and sat up straighter. Maybe it had given me courage. I'd better hang on to it.

When the bus screeched to a stop, Rosie Velarde got on. Her dark hair was pulled back in a braid and her bangs made a neat line across her forehead. She was the only twelve-year-old I knew who could wear her hair like that and not look like a little kid. I'd known Rosie since second grade, but we'd never really hung out. Jilly thought she was stuck up, but I didn't. I was kind of afraid of her, though. She always said what she thought, and I wondered when she was going to say something about me.

Rosie stepped down the aisle, walking by without even looking at me. I slumped against the window, my forehead cooled by the glass. No one sat next to me for the entire ride to school.

• • •

Molly Brown Middle School was HUGE. The building was really four connected buildings that formed a big brown-bricked square with a courtyard in the middle. Each of the four buildings held classes of related subjects, which was supposed to be easier to navigate and make students feel "connected." It made me feel lost and trapped.

The tour we had two weeks ago did not help me find my way around. It was like a labyrinth, with doors and hallways that seemed to go nowhere. Hogwarts without the magic. Or the Forbidden Forest. MBMS had what I would call a Forbidden Hedge, an ugly row of junipers running the length of the front of the building where the buses let us off.

I was in no hurry to face a bunch of strangers, so I stayed in my seat on the bus, untying and retying my shoes, then rearranging the stuff in my backpack until the bus was nearly empty.

"So, where's Hennessey?"

I looked up to see Rosie Velarde standing next to my seat.

"She has strep."

"Bummer." Rosie adjusted her backpack straps over both shoulders and headed down the bus steps and out the door.

Why didn't she stay when she saw that Jilly wasn't here? What about being a Good Samaritan? We could have walked off the bus together. Maybe she was on my track. We could have walked to some classes together.

Maybe Jilly was right. Maybe Rosie Velarde was stuck up.

By the time I was actually off the bus and into the building, I was convinced Rosie was the most stuck-up girl in the entire universe. Right now she was probably in the hall somewhere, laughing an evil villain-like laugh as she imagined me wandering the halls alone, a neon LOSER flashing over my head.

• • •

I stumbled upon my homeroom just after the last bell rang, freezing in the doorway as twenty-five faces, all on time, stared at me. Rosie's was one of them. But she was smiling a Good Samaritan kind of smile, and I felt a little better.

My eyes skimmed over the freshly painted walls; the posters of Harriet Tubman, Sally Ride, Benjamin Franklin, and Cesar Chavez; the rows of bookshelves under the windows; and the two computers in the back corner. Seeing the backs of the monitors comforted me.

"You must be Miss Swift," the teacher said.

"You must be Ms. Archer."

"She's very swift," a boy in the second row said. A few kids chuckled. He was way cute but didn't look snotty or stuck up like most good-looking guys, which meant I would forgive the "swift" joke I'd heard a zillion times. His bangs were long and fell over one eye, and his nose had a few freckles sprinkled over it. The eye I could see was dark brown and looked right into mine. That kind of freaked me out. Most boys I knew never looked at you head-on; they always looked over your shoulder, as if they were really talking to someone behind you.

He sat next to Rosie Velarde, who smiled when Cute Boy nudged her. No fair. Did she know this guy?

Before I could continue my cuteness inventory, the teacher told me to sit down. I plopped down in the only available seat, which happened to be in the front row because no one in their right mind would want to sit in the front row, especially on the first day of school when you want to scope out your fellow inmates. I snuck a peek to my left and right. Oh, no. Not only was I in the dreaded front row, which was bad enough, but I was next to my favorite person in the whole world (not): Serena Worthington, aka Serena Worthlessness, or my personal favorite, Serena Poopendena. I couldn't even feel sorry for her for having a bad romance-novel name because she was such a snot. Her hair was perfectly combed and curled, hairspray holding it in place. *Blech*. I couldn't believe that there were two other tracks that Serena could have been on and she was on my track, in my homeroom. And

Jilly wasn't. I wondered if we would get to vote someone out of homeroom. I knew who I'd pick.

I scrunched my nose and crossed my eyes at Serena.

"You look uglier than usual when you do that thing with your face," Serena whispered loudly.

I did the mature thing. I stuck out my tongue.

"Nice," she said.

I pulled my tongue back in, angry at myself for letting her get to me. I decided right then and there that nothing, absolutely NOTHING, was going to get to me this first day at MBMS.

And Nothing's name was Serena Worthington.

chapter 3

Erin Swift, Puppet

My day began to crumble between fifth and sixth periods. I, the Crumblee, was leaving a stall in the girls' bathroom when I saw Serena, the Crumbler, at the sink, primping.

"How are you ever going to get by without Geppetto?" Serena said, reapplying her lip gloss and smacking her lips at herself in the mirror.

I should have ignored her, should have washed and waxed and left quickly. But no. I had to respond.

"What?" I stood behind her, hands on hips, Jilly's pin jabbing away at the funny little twinge I got when she said "Geppetto."

"*You* know," Serena said, turning to face me. She rubbed her lips together, smearing the lip gloss and sending a waft of berry my way. "Jillian is Geppetto, the master puppeteer, and you're Pinocchio." She leaned toward me. "The puppet."

Wham! A fist slammed into her face. It took me a second to realize it was mine. My throbbing knuckles set off the fire alarm. No wait, that wasn't the alarm; it was Serena's wailing, echoing and reverberating in the bathroom like a siren.

. . .

"Molly Brown Middle School does not tolerate violence of any kind," said Mrs. Josephine Porter, principal of MBMS.

I swallowed, wondering if I needed a lawyer but afraid to ask. My eyes darted around the room. Behind her desk, Mrs. Porter had a large *Sound of Music* poster and several puppets — hand puppets, marionettes, finger puppets — on racks in a corner. Having just been called one a few minutes before, I wasn't thrilled to see them all over her office.

"I see you've noticed my puppet collection," Mrs. Porter said, her voice softening. "They're such fun, aren't they?"

If she knew my pain, she couldn't possibly have asked that question. I said nothing.

"I'd like to hear you speak," said Mrs. Porter.

I had a sudden urge to bark. But I'd probably lose points for that. I held it back and managed a squeaky "yes" in response.

"I like puppets. Especially marionettes." Mrs. Porter sighed deeply, putting her chin in her hands.

Of all the principals on the planet, I had to get one who had a thing for puppets.

"Um, Mrs. Porter?" I asked. "What's going to happen to me?"

She straightened up and cleared her throat. "Well, that has yet to be decided. You are off on the wrong foot, Miss Swift, and I hope this is not indicative of what we can expect for the remainder of the term."

I almost pointed out that there wasn't a right foot with me, only a big one, but I didn't. "No, ma'am," I said. I looked at my hand. At first I thought I saw blood. Then I realized it was Serena's lip gloss. I rubbed it off. "Where's Serena?"

"Miss Worthington is being looked at by the school nurse."

I felt a pang of guilt. What if I broke her nose? Then I really would need a lawyer.

Mrs. Porter didn't say any more about Serena but proceeded to ask questions. The conversation was so strange, I wondered if perhaps I'd made it up. But my parents talked about it later, so I knew it had really happened. Here it is, word for crazy word.

<u>THE PORTER INQUISITION</u>

Place: The principal's neat but stuffy puppet-filled office

Time: Two o'clock

Players: Me, Mrs. Porter (Mrs. P), and later, my parents

<u>ACTION BEGINS</u>

Mrs. P: Why did you hit Miss Worthington?

Me: She called me something.

Mrs. P: She called you a name?

Me: (squirming in my seat) Sort of.

Mrs. P: Was it a — (turning a bit pink) — a derogatory name?

Me: You mean, like a cussword?

Mrs. P: (nods)

Me: No.

Mrs. P: Well, then, what was it?

Me: I'd rather not say.

Mrs. P: Oh. I see. (Which, of course, she didn't.)

Me: She called me a puppet, okay? Now, what's going to happen to me?

Mrs. P: A puppet?

Me: Yes. Did you call my parents?

Mrs. P: They are on their way. (Pause. Looks over shoulder at puppet collection.) What's wrong with being called a puppet?

Me: It was the way she said it, Mrs. Porter.

Mrs. P: Of course. Well, even so, we cannot tolerate violence of this kind.

I breathed a sigh of relief. At least she was back to talking about my crime. But when my parents got there, the first thing Mrs. Porter asked was whether they liked puppets.

"Puppets?" my dad asked. "I thought Erin hit someone in the girls' bathroom."

"Oh, she did," Mrs. Porter said. "And it was about puppets."

"It was not *about* puppets," I said. "She *called* me a puppet."

"You hit Serena Worthington for calling you a puppet?" my mom asked.

"It was the way she said it, Mrs. Swift," said Mrs. Porter.

"Oh. Of course," said my dad, giving me a wide-eyed "what the heck is going on?" look.

"Mrs. Porter?" my mom asked. "What is the school's policy on hitting?"

Because of my clean record in elementary school and the fact that Mrs. Porter (aka Puppet Porter) liked puppets, I got off with a light sentence — three days of detention. I had to apologize to Serena Poopendena, though, which was worse than detention. She sneered at me behind a big bag of ice, making me want to hit her again. Twice as hard.

And she didn't have to apologize for calling me a puppet, which was totally unfair.

"Totally," Jilly agreed when I showed up at her house after my parents drove me home. She was officially no longer contagious (too bad — I could have used a good bout of strep to keep me away from MBMS), and we hung out in her room, aka Diva Central. My eyes were always drawn to the different shades of pink swirling across the walls like the skirts of a dancer. I glanced at the poster of Meryl Streep ("an actor's actor") above her bed and checked the other poster across the room to see if her Movie Star Crush of the Month had changed this week.

Noting that it was still the same, I sat down in the chair at her desk, glancing at the array of photos pinned to her bulletin board. Many were of me and her, but some were of her and other friends I didn't really hang out with. A couple were family photos.

"So," said Jilly. "How big and purple was her nose?"

"You've seen Barney, right?"

We both laughed.

Jilly didn't like Serena either. In elementary school we kept track of every zit and blemish, as well as any potential die-of-embarrassment situations, such as boogers hanging out of her nose or red stains on her clothes. Serena was one of eight girls in last year's sixth grade who had started their periods, something Jilly and I couldn't even imagine. We were so glad we didn't have to worry about that stuff, but wouldn't mind the other stuff, like getting boobs. Too bad we couldn't get boobs without getting our period. They were sort of a package deal.

"Well," said Jilly, "at least it's over. By tomorrow no one will remember it."

I shook my head. "You weren't there when I got out of the principal's office." I unzipped my backpack. "Mrs. Porter had to talk to my parents alone, so I sat out on the bench, waiting. I don't know how many people called me 'puppet' or 'Pinocchio' when they walked by." And all because of stupid Serena. I hated her.

"No way," Jilly said.

"Way," I replied. "The gossip superhighway at Molly Brown is wireless."

"It's definitely faster than elementary school." Jilly opened the folder I'd dropped on the bed and pulled out the papers. "Homework on the first day? Give me a break."

"It's just a questionnaire," I said. "Everyone got one."

Jilly rolled her eyes. "Where are the maps?"

"They're in there." I'd gone over both her routes twice and drawn the maps carefully. Jilly held out one of them, taking steps around her room to practice. She would study them tonight and sail easily to each class as if she'd been doing it for years.

"Does this say 'lib,' as in library, or lab?"

"Library," I answered, without looking. Only one of the routes went past the library, and neither went by a lab. I could picture the turn in my mind. Heck, I knew her schedule better than mine. As I watched her walk, stop, and turn, studying the map I'd made her, I felt that funny twinge again. The same one I got when Serena had called me Pinocchio. But I couldn't quite identify it. Like when I'm trying to remember something I've forgotten and it's right there, just out of reach.

"I've got to go," I said suddenly, standing up.

"But we have to plan for tomorrow," Jilly protested. "And we need to fill out these questionnaires."

"I did mine already." It had helped me ignore all those people calling me names outside the principal's office. I had acted as if my life depended on filling in the answers for my name (Erin P. Swift), my interests (basketball, soccer, computers, having my best friend on the same track as me), and what I hoped to get out of my MBMS experience (to get out, period).

"But what about the bus?" Jilly asked, tapping the map with a polished fingernail. "I know. You come to my house and we'll walk together."

"Okay," I said, even though it made more sense for us to walk from my house, which was closer to the bus stop. Once that was decided, I practically ran from the room. The walls felt as if they had been pushed closer, like that trash compactor in the first *Star Wars,* which was really the fourth *Star Wars,* even though it was made first, and the first one was made fourth.

"Call me!" Jilly shouted.

I would. I always did.

my life

My Life | Mug Shots | MBMS | Snickers

Tuesday, August 20
5:00 p.m.

Ok, so I've decided to share 1 of my deep dark secrets from childhood. Since I'm 12¼, that isn't very long ago but it's still a deep dark secret so . . . no telling.

When I was younger and something horrible happened to me, I would hide in 1 of 5 different places, depending on the degree of horribleness of the situation. My brother, Chris, always had to come find me, so he named these spots. Of course, he had to explain to me that DEFCON was a military term, short for Defense Condition or Defense Readiness Condition, used when the U.S. was under some kind of military threat. I thought this fit my situations perfectly.

Here they are in order of least horrible to absolutely the MOST horrible of all:

DEFCON 5

My bed. I would throw myself on it when things were just a little bad . . . like when I tripped over my feet and no 1 saw me, but I still felt stupid.

DEFCON 4

The basement room closet, where I went when things were a little bit worse . . . like when Jilly gave me the same valentine she gave to Anna Pike in kindergarten . . . B4 I paid attention and saw that there were only 4 types of valentines in those shoe boxes.

▲ DEFCON 3

The neighbor's shed... a great hideout with their lawn tools and mower. I went there in 3rd grade when I farted in the girls' bathroom and Serena was in the stall next to me. You can guess the humiliation that came after.

▲ DEFCON 2

The bushes on the other side of the neighbor's house... pretty horrible stuff if I came here... like when Louis Barnes announced to the entire 2nd grade that my shoes could be the *Nina* and the *Pinta* for the school play. Jerk.

▲ DEFCON 1

The O'Learys' tree house at the end of the block... the ultimate horrible. Like when Serena put pudding on my chair in 4th grade and I sat in it and didn't know it right away and walked around with chocolate smeared on my shorts and everyone said I pooped in my pants. Jerkette.

What happened today – the Puppet Incident (aka the PI) – definitely DEFCON 1... but the tree house was packed with kids. I headed for DEFCON 5... more comfortable.

So my brother comes banging on my door today and I'm thinking he's just checking on me like he used to when I had a DEFCON thing... but get this. He starts YELLING at me about hitting Serena... I'm like, what is that all about? Well, I'll tell you what it's all about. He's CRAZY. Turns out he likes Serena's older sister, Amanda... convinced that she'll never look at him, let alone like him, when she finds out I'm the 1 who hit Serena.

Excuse me? If she's like Serena, he should be THANKING me... but no... he called me a loser and said I was the only person on the planet who could ruin someone's life from a distance. Can you believe that? What a jerk.

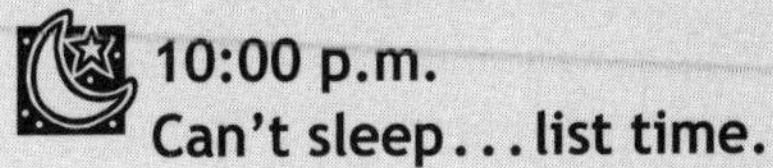
10:00 p.m.
Can't sleep... list time.

Things That Stink 

- Humiliation by She Who Doesn't Deserve to Be Named Even Though She Has a Stupid Romance Novel Name and People Should Be Making Fun of HER.

- She Who Doesn't Deserve to Be Named was snotty to me at lunch, B4 the PI—"Poor Erin. No Jilly, no 1 to sit with." When I told her I was meeting someone outside, she didn't believe me. I wasn't, but so what? I absolutely HATE that she didn't believe me. (See below for how it turned out. I actually did meet someone outside. Poop on you, S.W.)

- Cute Boy—aka Mark Sacks—will never talk to me again cuz no 1 that cute would ever be around a large-footed puppet who hits people in the nose.

Why I'm Not Losing All Hope 

- Rosie said hi back when I said hi after homeroom.

- This really quiet girl named Carla is my locker partner... seems nice.

Ok, so here's why my not meeting anyone at lunch turned out to be meeting someone at lunch. 1st, I had to sneak outside cuz there was nowhere to sit without letting people know I had no 1 to sit with... but then a miracle happened. I met my word processing teacher, Ms. Moreno. She told me about an Intranet Club that she's starting. I didn't even know what an Intranet was. I guess it's like the Internet, only private, like only in a company or school. She said it will only be faculty, students, and staff who can access the MBMS Intranet. How cool is that? A mini-Internet right in your own school!

But the coolest thing was when she went back inside with me. In the cafeteria, she handed me a piece of paper and asked me to look it over, like I was helping her out on some project or something. Lots of kids saw and looked at us—is that cool or what?

- Ms. Moreno understands my pain.

- I've got this Web Club Intranet thingie.

- Jilly is still my friend, even though she cared more about learning the map to her classes than she did about the PI.

Why is it that the things that stink are WAY bigger than the things that give me hope?

P.S. This is the longest entry in the history of blogging . . . I wonder if I can get in the *Guinness Book*.

chapter 4

Pinocchio Stalls

"Have you come up with a plan to get us on the same track?" I asked Jilly the next morning when I picked her up at her house.

Jilly shook her head. "Not yet. But something will come up." She dug in her backpack and pulled out some Tic Tacs. "I got these for you."

"Is that a hint?" I asked, fingering my own package of Tic Tacs in my pocket.

Jilly laughed. "No. Your breath never smells bad. I just got you one when I got my supply." She unzipped her backpack further to reveal about ten boxes of Tic Tacs. "You never know when you'll be talking face-to-face with a cute boy."

"Right," I said, thinking that if I was ever face-to-face with a cute boy (not to mention Cute Boy), I'd need more than a Tic Tac because I'd probably barf from fear.

Jilly kind of bounced as she walked. She looked excited, like she was going to Six Flags or the mall, not to MBMS. She reached over and squeezed my arm. "Here we go."

Yep. Here we go. Right into the mean-kid-infested jungle.

Before we reached the bus stop, she stopped me. "Sniff test," she whispered. I rolled my eyes but leaned over and sniffed quickly above her shoulder to make sure she didn't smell.

"Fine," I said.

"Other one," Jilly commanded, twisting at the waist. Eye roll, sniff.

All done. I had refused to sniff under her arm the way she had asked me to do the first time she wore deodorant in fifth grade.

"You're disgusting," I had told her.

"You're my friend," she'd replied, pouting.

"Will you sniff under my arm?" I lifted it high and leaned toward her.

"Well, no." She pulled back. "All right, all right. You don't have to do under the arm. But above my shoulder, okay? I just can't tell by myself."

I never made her sniff above my shoulders. I trusted Secret to keep my BO secrets a secret. Of course, when I got on the bus, my pores opened wide and not even the Hoover Dam could have stopped the flood.

"Hey, look. It's Pinocchio!" someone shouted.

"How's that right hook?" said a boy in the back.

"I can't believe you're famous after one day," Jilly said as we plopped down in the very front seat, behind the bus driver.

"Famous for being a puppet." Before Jilly could respond, a boy across the aisle leaned over.

"You must be Geppetto," he said.

Jilly rolled her eyes, but I could tell she liked the attention. "My name is Jillian," she said. "Not Geppetto."

"Okay, Jillian-not-Geppetto." The boy grinned at her and she smiled back before turning to give me Big Eyes, which meant *Can you believe this guy?* She was loving it.

Jilly talked a mile a minute beside me, which helped me ignore the name calling. When we got to school, I dropped Jilly off at her locker and ran to the other side of the school to my locker. The first thing I noticed when I got there was Mark Sacks, aka Cute Boy, pointing at something on the wall. My eyes followed his finger. It was a picture of Pinocchio with a face glued over Pinocchio's and a very long foot in the place of Pinocchio's nose. It wasn't my foot, but it was my face. From the elementary school yearbook. Jilly had wanted to see what I'd look like with a beard, so she painted my chin with chocolate ice cream. Of course the photo made it into the yearbook. And now someone had enlarged it and plastered it on the wall of Molly Brown Middle School.

I stood there with my mouth hanging open. Then Rosie stopped next to Mark. They both looked at the picture. Rosie glanced my way, but I turned before our eyes met.

"Swift!" It was Mark. I turned and hurried down the hall. I didn't want to hear his jokes.

When I got to my locker, it had another picture taped to it, along with Silly String covering the entire front. I ripped the picture down and pulled off the Silly String as I opened the locker door. String was everywhere inside, too, thanks to the locker vents. Tears stung my eyes, but I blinked them away as I peeled the string off my stuff. Then I started on my locker partner's.

"Don't worry about it." Carla's voice startled me. "I can get it."

"I'm sorry," I said, turning my face so she couldn't see how close I was to crying. I hustled to class, passing another Pinocchio picture on the way. Someone had written a message across the huge foot: FEET APPEAR SMALLER THAN ACTUAL SIZE. I grimaced. Ripping down the picture, I stuffed it into a trash can, imagining I was stuffing Serena's face into the candy wrappers, sticky ABC gum, and, with any luck, a half-eaten Twinkie with the cream nice and moldy and ready for wearing.

When I got to my word processing class, Ms. Moreno smiled encouragingly at me. She seated us in alphabetical order, and when Mark sat down in front of me, he tried to catch my eye. I pretended my mouse needed cleaning.

Suddenly his face appeared above my monitor.

"Don't say a word," I hissed.

"I wasn't —"

"That's two words," I said. "Three if you want to get technical about the contraction."

Mark sighed, shook his head, and faced front. I could only imagine the puppet jokes I had just saved myself from.

Hurrying from class to class, I endured constant shouts of "Pinocchio!" "Hey, Pinoke!" but I ignored them. I'd been teased about my feet. I could handle this.

At least I thought I could.

After lunch someone attached string to my back, which I didn't notice until a girl I didn't know pulled on it, talking in a fakey doll-like voice. "My name is Erin. I have big feet. I want to be a real boy." What I wanted was to scream in her face. Instead, I ripped the string off and ran into the girls' bathroom, locking myself in a stall. I fought back tears as I leaned against one wall, breathing in the sharp scent of ammonia as I wondered how in the world I was going to survive the rest of the week, let alone seventh grade, with a start like this.

Moaning, I sat down on the toilet, clutching Jilly's pin in my hand as the door to the bathroom smacked open.

"Poor Serena," said one girl. Leaning over, I looked through the crack in the stall. It was two girls Poopendena hung out with.

"She won't even let me in her house," said the other. "I stood on her front porch and talked to her through the door."

"That Erin Swift," the first one said. I sat up straighter. "I can't believe she did that. She's so —"

"She's a loser," interrupted the second girl. "Without Jillian, she's nobody. Did you hear Jillian is on Track C and Erin's on A Track? Swift is on her own."

My cheeks burned. I knew I should burst out of the stall, shouting, yelling . . . something. But I couldn't. I closed my fist tighter around the pin, letting the sharp point poke into my palm. I just wanted them to go away. I just wanted everyone to leave me alone.

They shuffled across the floor in my direction. My heart raced. What if they looked under the door? I glanced down at my ratty red Chuck Taylors. They'd know my feet.

Pulling my Chucks back on either side of the toilet, I prayed they wouldn't check. When they passed my stall, I sighed with relief and leaned slightly to the left to peek at them through the narrow gap between the door and the stall. They were drying their hands with paper towels.

"Someone already took down the pictures," one girl whined. "And after all that work."

I smiled. Jilly. Nanny-nanny boo-boo on them.

The restroom door opened again and the two girls stopped talking. I shifted my weight to see who came in, but she was just out of my sight line.

The first girl lowered her voice but I could still hear her. "I bet some people will say mean things about the way she looks when she comes back."

"She deserved it." I recognized that voice.

"You think everyone deserves it, Velarde."

"Nope," said Rosie. "Just her." I heard footsteps coming closer. "She's like a tick in a dog's ear. That's what my grandma would say. Of course, she'd say it in Spanish, which you wouldn't understand." I heard feet shuffling. "She doesn't have to be so mean to everyone."

"She's not mean to everyone," the first girl protested. "And I can't believe you called her a tick. I'm going to tell her."

Rosie snorted. "Oooh. I'm scared." Her voice was low, near the floor. She was checking under the stalls! I backed up as far as I could as the stall door beside mine opened and closed. I held my breath, wondering if Rosie had seen my feet. A few seconds later I got my answer.

A hand appeared suddenly on my side of the stall, waving its fingers. I wondered if it was a friendly, how-ya-doing wave, or a I-won't-blow-your-cover-but-you-owe-me wave. It didn't really matter, though. I was so grateful for those wiggling fingers. I reached out to them, wanting to hold onto them. But just as quickly as they appeared, they were gone.

And then I wondered if I'd seen them at all.

S.W. Hate-o-Rama

My Life | Mug Shots | MBMS | S.W. Hate-o-Rama | Snickers

Yes, this is a brand-new page with its very own link. Why, you may ask? Cuz after Rosie wiggled her fingers at me, after I survived my 1st day of detention and went back to my locker, I found a stuffed puppet sitting there, covered with mud and gunk. Someone had propped up a sign that said: ERIN SWIFT, QUEEN OF THE PUPPETS. Spent the next 15 minutes cleaning up...didn't tell Mom why I was late getting out to the car...should have shown Puppet Porter how some people don't respect puppets.

Of course the meanest girl in the whole world did this...not her exactly cuz she wasn't in school today. Even if she was, she'd be 2 chicken to do it herself. She had her stupid friends do it. Jerkettes of the World.

So, cuz of this latest horrible thing and cuz I HATE HER, S.W. gets her very own HATE-O-RAMA web page. Isn't she lucky.

Public Enemy #1

[Note to self: insert ugliest photo in the world of S.W.]

Serena Worthington, aka Serena Poopendena, Serena Snottington, Serena the Teenage B----.

Things I Hate About PE #1

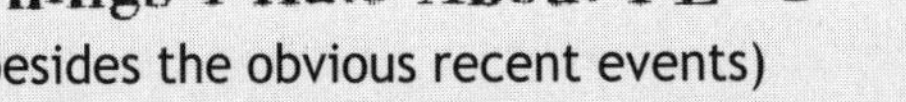

(besides the obvious recent events)

- She's already 13 and thinks she's hot stuff.
- She already has some boobs, not just pokies.

- Some people like her even though she's not a nice person. (What's wrong with them?)

- She called me names and didn't get in trouble (that sticks and stones thing is a bunch of poopola).

Revenge Ideas

- Cut off all of her hair, including her eyelashes.

- Throw her into the Forbidden Hedge.

- Spit in her soup.

- Find out which boy she likes and tell him that her mom was the bearded lady in a small circus and it's only a matter of time B4 her beard starts growing 2.

Random Thoughts

Rosie thinks Serena is an annoying tick in a dog's ear...she's worse than a tick...a mosquito, poking at people, sucking their blood, and leaving a bad itch behind.

Chris is giving me the ST (Silent Treatment) cuz his prediction was right. Amanda apparently went off on him about me hitting Serena and told him that only a real jerk would have a sister like that. Hello? I tried to tell him that someone who would blame him for something I did was probably not worth it, but he acted like I hadn't said anything. How rude is that? Here I am suffering extreme humiliation and pain, and I found it in my heart to reach out to my brother. What does he do? He rebuffs me. (Just read this word today. Isn't it great?)

Click here to ban Pinocchio signs and references from all public buildings.

Click here to throw virtual darts at S.W.'s face.

Click here to contribute your own Revenge of the Puppet Ideas.

Click here for a reenactment of the Insult and the Punch (must have a video player plug-in).

Click here if you are tired of clicking and just want a Snickers.

chapter 5

What's Your Sign?

I survived my three days of detention and slogged through the next several averaging about six to ten puppet-related jokes a day. Then, the day of PON (Parent Orientation Night), exactly one week and one day after the PI, I was saved by a kiss.

"A janitor caught two eighth graders making out in one of the second-floor closets!" The news spread like a computer virus, and everyone forgot about Erin the Puppet. It was like magic. Like one of those fairy tales where the prince wakes up the princess with a kiss. Except in this case the princess was wide awake and mashing right back.

"I would never pick a janitor's closet," said Jilly on the bus ride home. "All those cleaner smells? How not romantic."

I couldn't imagine kissing a boy I liked, let alone the actual place I might do such a thing, so I just stayed quiet, enjoying the fact that everyone was talking and none of it was about me. I smiled as I glanced out the window. If I could find those eighth graders, I'd kiss them.

"So, play tryouts are September 25," Jilly said. "I signed us both up."

"Already?"

"They'll see our names up there every day for the next few weeks," she said. "They'll remember us."

I didn't want to be remembered. But I always tried out with Jilly.

"I picked up a couple of scripts for us." Jilly pulled out two thin booklets. “I’m trying out for Goody Morgan,” she said. “You should try out for Constance. She’s my neighbor.”

Constance had five lines in the play. I’d never had more than one. I didn’t want to be Constance. I didn’t want to be anyone. I just wanted to work on the computer and play basketball. I looked over at Jilly. Maybe I’d tell her the truth.

“Oh, Erin, I’m so excited!” Jilly said. “To think we’ll get to be in another play together. That’s the best part, don’t you think? Doing it together?”

I closed my mouth, so the words I was going to say disappeared and new ones came out.

“Sure, Jilly. That’s the best part.”

• • •

“You signing up for the Intranet Club?” Mark was talking to Rosie, who sat on her desk in homeroom, balancing a pen on the tip of her finger. I sat down and faced front, listening to their conversation as I pulled my books out of my backpack.

“Yeah,” she said. “Someone’s got to make sure you don’t look bad.”

Mark laughed. “Very funny.” *Zing.* Something hit the back of my neck. “What about you?” A small wad of paper dropped to the ground as I turned around.

“You’re lucky that wasn’t a spitball,” I said.

“I’m lucky? You mean you’re lucky.” He wadded up another piece of paper and tossed it my way. “So, are you?”

I was about to answer when I felt Rosie looking at me.

“Is Jilly signing up?” she asked.

“I’m going to ask her this afternoon, but I don’t think she will.”

“But you’re signing up, right?” Mark was looking right at me, as if he really did want me to sign up.

I nodded.

Rosie raised her eyebrows but didn't say anything, then turned to Mark. "I'll meet you at our usual spot for lunch. I already have homework."

I had a feeling I knew what she was thinking, but it bugged me too much to think about it. I pulled out a notebook and drew pictures of myself with small feet until the bell rang.

• • •

I tried to bring up the Intranet Thing with Jilly on the bus, but she was too busy talking about some new girls she'd met and wondering if they'd try out for the play, too. When we got to her house to do our homework, I was forced to talk about it because when I pulled out my books, the Intranet Club flyer floated to the ground at her feet.

"You aren't going to do that computer club, are you?" she asked, setting her backpack on her chair. "I mean, I know you like computers and all but . . . boring." She faked a yawn and looked at herself in the mirror hanging above her dresser, fluffing her bangs.

"I was thinking about it," I said. "What if we did it together, like the play?"

"I don't want to do it, Erin. You know I don't know my Shift key from my house key."

"Home key," I corrected. "It's the Home key."

"See? Whatever," she said. "I just don't want to do it." She unzipped her backpack and pulled out her homework. Actually, even though I was scared to do something without her, I was glad she didn't want to. If she joined the Club, she'd see Mark and if she saw Mark she'd like him instantly and he'd like her and that would be that. If there hadn't been a Mark factor, I would have pushed harder, telling her how the ratio of boys to girls would probably be five to one in the Intranet Club. But there was the Mark factor, so I didn't push.

"Well," I said, feeling my heart speed up a bit, "I think I'd like to do it."

Jilly glanced over at me. "Without me?"

"It would be weird without you, but I'd still like to do it."

Jilly's eyes returned to her books. She tugged them out of her backpack one at a time.

"It's not like I'm going to tell you what to do, Erin, but you need to make sure it isn't going to get in the way of the play." She paused. "And doing homework together and stuff."

"It won't," I said. I shifted on her bed, feeling irritated. *What about things getting in the way of the Intranet Club?* I thought. But I didn't say it out loud.

Jilly sighed. "I'll miss going home on the bus with you on those days."

"I'll miss that, too." I smiled, the irritation slipping away. "Thanks." I wasn't sure what I was thanking her for, but it seemed like the right thing to say.

Wednesday, August 28

Ok, here's something embarrassing. I almost pulled a table down on top of myself in front of Cute Boy. It happened at PON last night....stopped by the Intranet Club table while my parents went to my homeroom to hear all about my classes...Ms. Moreno and Mr. Arnett started telling me all about the Club and how they only can take 25 people and then they both had to leave so Ms. Moreno asked if I could watch the table. Mark comes up, so I tried to hide my feet by holding onto the edge of the table and sliding them under. WHAM...almost went down. SO embarrassing.

Serena came by and made some stupid comment...stuck my tongue out at her. She totally likes Mark, but I don't think I can tell him that her mom is the bearded lady in a small circus...unless I can see that he likes her 2. Don't think he does cuz he just kind of shook his head and rolled his eyes at her.

Mark told me he finally reached the last level in *Space Invaders*, which freaked me out cuz I thought I was the only one who played the new version of "the old favorite" as my dad calls it...didn't tell him that I'd reached the final level in 2nd grade...just smiled and said that was cool, afraid my heart might burst out through my mouth and bonk him on the head or something...it was crazy inside my chest, like it was trapped in a cage, desperate to get out.

Chris is still mad at me, BUT Mark Sacks TALKED to me. Me, Erin P. Swift. WAHOO!!!!!!!!!!

chapter 6

Making My Mark

I decided it was time to do something about my friend situation, which was basically nonexistent. At the door of the cafeteria the next day, I stared out into the vastness, wondering how all of these people could possibly look like they belonged. The tables were round to "promote feelings of connectedness," according to the information my parents had received. But all it did was show even more clearly who had friends and who didn't, and made it more obvious when you walked up to a table for a seat because everyone could see you at a round table. If the tables were rectangular, like in a normal cafeteria, you could stand at one end where no one was sitting and act like you were looking elsewhere, even if you were scoping out that table. That was practically impossible with round tables.

I squared my shoulders, took the biggest, hugest breath I could take, and walked right up to the table where Rosie and Mark were sitting.

"Anybody sitting here?" I indicated the spot next to Rosie.

Rosie shook her head but didn't look up from her noodles. I sat down, listening to Mark and Rosie talk about their families. I found out that Mark used to live next to Rosie's aunt and they would hang out together when Rosie's family visited. *She's known him forever,* I thought. *No wonder they're such good friends.*

"So," Rosie said after taking a bite of pasta. "Why are you sitting here?"

Rosie had always been straightforward and to the point, but she'd never been straightforward and to the point with me.

"Um," I said. She didn't say anything. "Um," I said again. And then, "Remember the time you stuffed Play-Doh in Kevin Hudson's mouth when he made fun of my feet?"

There was a hint of a smile on Rosie's face. "You remember that?"

"How could I not? He gagged so much he almost threw up." I laughed. "Besides, when someone stands up for you, you remember."

"I'm sure Jilly stands up for you all the time." Rosie took a sip of her water.

I shrugged. "I guess." Mark was talking to a boy next to him so I leaned over, speaking quietly. "You wiggled your fingers at me in the bathroom. On the second day of school. Thanks."

Rosie took another bite of her noodles.

I waited. Why wasn't she saying anything?

"Why are you watching me eat?"

"I'm not!" My cheeks warmed.

"Yes, you were."

"Okay, I was," I said. "I'm just trying to figure out what's up with you."

Rosie chewed slowly and deliberately. Then she looked right at me. "If Jilly were here, right now, would you be sitting with me? Would you be talking to me?"

Wow. To the point. I frowned. "I hope so."

"But you're not sure?"

I shook my head.

"Well, at least you're honest."

We finished our lunches, talking about the play — Rosie: Why in the world would you try out for that? Me: I don't know. — and the possibilities of the Intranet Club.

Rosie acted like we hadn't even had that weird part of the conversation, but it flitted in the air around us the whole time. Would I try to be friends with Rosie if Jilly and I were together on the same track?

I had a feeling I knew the answer. And I didn't like it.

• • •

I stood at my locker, hands on hips, looking as if I couldn't find something. But out of the corner of my eye I was watching Mark at his locker. I hadn't said anything to him at lunch. I was determined to say something brilliant and witty this afternoon.

I grabbed my locker door and kept staring inside. If I timed it right, I could close my locker just as he was about to pass me and maybe we could walk to class together. Wow. I couldn't believe I was planning that way. But I was.

A boy sauntered over and leaned against the lockers next to Mark, blocking my view. I leaned out to get a better look. Suddenly, he peered around his locker door. I ducked so he wouldn't see me staring, banging my head on one of the coat hooks.

"Dang," I muttered, rubbing my brow with my fingers. Lifting my head, I put my eye against the slit between the door and my locker and scanned the hall. I leaned in, pulling the door along with me to get a different angle. Mark's locker was closed. He was gone.

Straightening up, I grabbed the locker door and closed it — finding myself face (mine) to shoulder (his) with Mark Sacks.

I sucked in my breath. I could feel my eyes widening to big-screen size.

"Um — um —" So much for brilliant and witty. I tried to smile. My face was only about a foot away from Mark's. I could see flecks of dark in the one gray eye. I could see all of his freckles running across his nose like so many dots. Then I freaked. What if I had bad breath? I didn't have my usual Tic Tac after lunch. What had I had for lunch anyway? Peanut butter. Did that smell bad on your breath? What if it was mixed with jelly and a little mashed banana? Banana peels stank if you left them in the car too long and it got hot. Maybe once they were hot inside your stomach, they stank, too. Maybe —

"Erin?" Mark interrupted my maybes.

"Huh?"

"I said I didn't see your name on the list. For the Intranet Club."

"You didn't?" I asked stupidly. "Oh, well, that's because I haven't signed up. Yet."

"Ms. Moreno said you're a real computer whiz so she'll probably hold a spot for you, but you may want to sign up just in case."

"She did?" No one had ever said that about me before.

"Yeah," said Mark. He was looking at me, not around me. This was my chance for brilliant and witty.

"So." I fell into step beside him, very aware of my feet, which seemed to loom extra large across the tile. "This cool sounds pretty club," I said nervously. "Have you ever webbed any feet before?" My stomach dropped. Had I just asked Mark Sacks if he'd webbed any feet?

Mark laughed. "I think I know what you mean," he said. "You're pretty funny."

I smiled, but inside the gymnastics continued. I wasn't trying to be funny. I was trying to ask a simple question about web design. What was wrong with me?

"I've done some web stuff," he said. "What about you?"

I took a deep breath, saying my answer once in my mind before saying it out loud. "My mom's a web designer. I help her out sometimes." I didn't tell him about my personal-private-no-one-will-see-but-me website.

"Lucky you," he said. "Do you know HTML?"

"Some. My mom has showed me some basic stuff. But she uses

Dreamweaver to design, which is totally over my head," I said. "I use FrontPage."

"Cool. I took a camp this summer and learned a bunch of codes, but I probably won't remember any of them."

I smiled, hoping it wasn't a goofy, lovey-dovey smile. I just wanted it to be a hey-we're-cool smile. I was having a normal conversation with Mark Sacks, with Cute Boy, and I hadn't done anything clumsy or stupid since my first webbed-foot question. And I wasn't worried about my feet. Then I wished I hadn't thought that because now I probably jinxed it.

"I'm sure you'll remember all of them and make the rest of us look stupid," I said.

"Doubtful." He stopped at the drinking fountain. Oh, dear. What should I do? Should I wait? Or was this his way of ending the conversation? I took a few steps forward. "Hold up," he said. Moments later he was back at my side. We talked a little more about computers until we got to class. I caught Serena staring at us as we entered, and I turned to Mark and laughed. Eat your heart out, Poopendena.

Tuesday, September 3

Questions to Ponder

- Would I be friends with Rosie if Jilly and I were on the same track?

  No.

- Do I like this answer?

  No.

- What will I do about this?

  Be Rosie's friend for real. Cuz that's what I want.

- Why haven't I asked Jilly if she has a plan for switching tracks?

  2 words: Mark Sacks.

- Why haven't I even THOUGHT about asking Jilly if she has a plan for switching tracks?

  See above.

- Am I ok with not switching tracks?

  Yes. (Omigosh)

chapter 7

Ace of Clubs

I stood outside Ms. Moreno's computer lab, tapping my left Chuck nervously as I stared down the hallway. I wasn't quite ready to go in. This was the first time I'd signed up for something without Jilly. And even though I didn't want her to be here because of the MF (Mark Factor), it had been strange writing my name on a list without Jilly's name right before it. Besides, there were a bunch of eighth graders in the Club, too. They probably knew way more than I did and would make me feel stupid.

"Don't tell me Hennessey's coming. She doesn't know anything about computers." My head jerked up at the voice. Ah. Serena Worthington's familiar scowl.

I shook my head.

Serena's eyes widened in mock surprise. "You signed up for this all by yourself? Without Geppetto? Wow. Maybe you will be a real boy."

"Shut up."

"Why are standing out here? Afraid to go in by yourself?" She shook her head. "Poor Baby Ewin." She said it in a baby voice, with "Ewin" instead of "Erin." I scowled.

"Can't you just be quiet?" Rosie walked up behind Serena, hitching up her backpack. Mark was with her.

"Well, she's standing out here like a loser, Velarde."

Rosie harrumphed. "She was waiting for us. Not that it's any of your business."

Serena looked at Mark, whose eyes shifted to Rosie. Then she turned to me. "Why didn't you say anything?" she asked. "Or do you still need someone to speak for you? Like those ventriloquists . . . with their dummies." She leaned toward me as she said the word "dummies," just begging me to punch her in the nose again. I could feel the heat rise in my cheeks. Why was Mark here? Why did he have to see Serena being so mean to me?

"Serena!" One of her friends called to her from down the hall. Serena rolled her eyes at us and looked back. I had that weird twinge again as the girl walked by, her eyes on Serena, waiting to hear what Serena would say. My throat closed up and I couldn't breathe, like when I was in Jilly's room that first day after school.

"What a snot," Mark said when Serena had gone into the lab. "Hey, Swift, are you okay?"

I nodded, unable to speak.

"I'm going to get a seat," Mark said, and he stepped inside the lab.

"I owe you one," I said to Rosie. Sighing, I shook my head. "I was a little scared to go in by myself."

"So what?" Rosie said. "It's no big deal."

I smiled, gathering my courage. "I thought about what you said." Rosie waited. "And here's my answer. Honestly? I probably would not be friends with you if Jilly were on this track. Honestly Number Two? I'm actually glad she isn't because I never would have gotten to know you or Mark." I knew it was true the moment I said it. I was actually glad we were on different tracks. I was.

"That's cool." Rosie nodded. "Okay, you go in first."

I looked at her, took a breath, and stepped through the doorway.

"Erin, good to see you." Ms. Moreno greeted me with a smile. "Sit wherever you want for now. I'll be having experienced kids, like you, lead groups for those who are new at this."

That got my attention. Me? Lead a group?

"You can do it," Ms. Moreno said, as if reading my mind. Rosie squeezed my shoulder as she swept past me to snag a chair next to Mark.

I made a face as if to say "I don't think so," then turned my attention to the room. Looking at the five clusters of five computers each, monitors shining, mice and trackballs waiting for eager fingers, I couldn't help smiling a little. I supposed having computers in a circle was going to "promote connectedness," too, though in this case it might work. Being able to look over the monitor at someone's face, rather than at the back of a head the way we did in word processing class, seemed like a good thing.

The back wall had a low row of shelves beneath the windows where computer manuals, paper, and games were shoved in at different angles. I cringed at the sight of a game disc without its case. You can't treat discs like that; they can scratch and get ruined. On the left wall hung a poster detailing the rules for safe surfing and another explained how to earn points to play different games.

"Ms. Moreno?" Serena, sitting in a cluster near the windows, had her hand in the air.

"Yes?"

"Are we going to have a gossip column? Or an advice column? I could do that."

Ms. Moreno stopped in front of her desk. "We'll talk about content in a few weeks. First we need to get everyone up to speed on how to create web pages." She picked up a stack of handouts and held them out to me. "Could you pass these out, please?"

"Sure." I pulled off my backpack and set it on an empty chair. Jilly's pin shifted in my pocket as I leaned over. Pulling it out, I looked at it briefly. I rubbed my fingers across the tape, which had rolled back to reveal part of the tragedy face. I put the pin halfway back in my pocket. Then I saw Rosie. She smiled at me and gave me the thumbs-up before looking down at her computer screen. I stuffed Jilly's pin into an outside pocket of my backpack, out of sight, out of touch, and delivered the handouts.

"This handout has some of the most common HTML commands," Ms. Moreno said as I returned to my seat. "We're going to start there. I want you to learn the commands and how they work before using software that does the work for you."

A few kids groaned, but I was excited. I figured I knew enough to tell people about it. Even though I used FrontPage, I often worked on the coding page so I could practice HTML.

"— will be with Erin Swift." My eyes shot up. I hadn't been listening. She must have been assigning groups. "Erin, will you raise your hand so people know where to go?" I lifted my hand slowly in the air, my eyes darting from kid to kid to see who was coming over. So far, no one I knew. Good. Maybe they wouldn't —

"I'm supposed to learn web design from Big Foot?" A boy sat down right next to me and crossed his arms over his chest. He had spiky hair and dark brown eyes. I saw part of a chain coming out from the collar of his T-shirt. He obviously thought he had the cool look down, but he was way too skinny and his voice cracked at the end of his question.

I turned and glared at him. "You can p align your butt to a different group," I said. "It doesn't matter to me."

"Huh?"

"P align is an HTML code for aligning something on a page." I looked up to see Mark Sacks standing in the cluster to our right, looking at the boy beside me. "Positioning it. You know, like left, center, right." He moved his hands to demonstrate each position. "She knows her stuff," he said, nodding at me. Then he turned and waved his group over, and they all sat down.

I had to bite the inside of my cheek to keep from grinning like a crazy girl. Cute Boy had said I knew my stuff! It felt like I grew two feet taller in two seconds. I looked down at my Chucks. Were they smaller and farther away now? Wahoo! Confidence surged through me as I turned to Mr. Spiky Hair.

"So?" I asked. "Are you staying or going?"

He looked at me for a moment. His eyes shifted to Mark's back, then returned to me. He sighed and picked up the handout. "What does HTML mean, anyway?"

"Hypertext Markup Language," I said. "Let me show you how it works."

Thursday, September 12

I Am Web Designer, See Me Code

Of course, I didn't tell the guy in the Intranet Club on Tues. what HTML really stands for: Hot Tamale Mark Love. I definitely have Hot Tamale Love for Mark Sacks. Rosie got me started on the hot tamale part. That's what she calls good-looking boys. She doesn't know about the Mark part.

I can't stop thinking about him... keep telling myself he's just my friend, he's just my friend, but can't seem to stop thinking, I wish he was my boyfriend, I wish he was my boyfriend.

Ok, Erin, QUIT IT.

Went over to Jilly's to do homework after school. She was playing fashion model while I was doing math cuz she couldn't decide what to wear. I'm like, why in the world are you asking me? You're the fashion queen. She said she was desperate, which made us both laugh.

I guess she's got this girl in 2 of her classes who is Miss Popular... the usual instant hate girl—blond, some boobage, etc.... but this 1 is also smart, Jilly says, which really has her freaked out.

I told Jilly she was smart, which was kind of true. Jilly is smart, but she does just enough to get by, so her grades don't really show how smart she is.

Anyway, she finally got her oldest sister, Becca, in the room. Becca is the Fashion Empress to Jilly's Fashion Queen... Tried to concentrate on my homework but I couldn't. Jilly freaking out was freaking me out.

Had to go home early... just couldn't watch anymore.

chapter 8

CORN-ered

Intranet Club was the BEST. My group hung on every word I said and learned HTML really fast. We were already putting some pages together because it turned out I knew the most about web design. Even more than the eighth graders. Our group was in charge of the "School Life" section, which included stuff like faculty interviews, awards, and a page called "A Day in the Life" where we profiled a few kids, then typed up a journal, which everyone would get to read once the Intranet was live online.

The only boring thing we had to do was list the courses and descriptions offered at MBMS, as well as the schedules for each track. But that only had to be done once, which was nice.

It also turned out that I was a pretty good leader when I knew what I was talking about. A couple of the eighth graders even asked me questions. And Tyler, formerly known as the Boy Who Wouldn't Take Instruction From Big Foot, was really into it and seemed to have forgotten all about thinking I was a dork. He asked me all kinds of questions and told me how smart I was.

"It's only because my mom's a web designer," I said modestly.

"Nah," Tyler said. "Even if both my parents were web designers, I wouldn't know the stuff you do."

I just smiled and showed him how to change the font size in his heading.

Mark's group was in charge of school events — arts and music, sports, and such. Not only did they list the events but they had reviewers and sportswriters covering each one. They had set it up like a newspaper, with digital photos and everything. Very cool.

"I can't log on. Why can't I log on?" Rosie sat at her computer, tapping angrily at the keyboard. "I have to get the letters to the editor ready by the end of the week." Rosie was in a group with an eighth-grade team leader, and they were in charge of all correspondence we received. This could be letters to the editor, letters for the weekly "Tell Us About It" column, or webmaster comments or complaints. Since we weren't going live until just before Thanksgiving, we asked a few kids to write in with questions or comments, and Rosie would include these in her first "Tell Us About It" column. Once we were live and the whole school had access to the Intranet, any student could send in a question or comment.

"We need a different name," I said during our break. Mark, Rosie, Tyler, and I were heading for the gym to shoot baskets. "'Intranet Club' is boring."

"Yeah," said Mark. "What about Web Club? We could be the Webbies."

"The Webbies?" Rosie, Tyler, and I said it at the same time, raising our eyebrows at him.

"Okay, so that was stupid," Mark said, laughing.

"What about the I-Club?" I said. "The letter I."

"The I-Club," Rosie said. "Cool."

"People might think we're reading eye charts and stuff," Mark said.

"Not people in the know," I said.

"Right," said Tyler.

There were a few kids in the gym when we got there. Rosie was a decent player, Tyler was horrible, and Mark and I were pretty even.

"I'm better at web design," Tyler gasped when Rosie and I beat him and Mark in a two-on-two game.

I laughed, and Rosie and I high-fived each other. "Is there anything you're not good at?" she asked as we headed back to the lab. I was so shocked I stopped right in my tracks and Tyler nearly bumped into me.

"Watch where you're stopping." Tyler grabbed my shoulders briefly from behind before stepping around me, grinning as he passed.

"Sorry," I said. He and Mark walked ahead of us, but I stayed put. Rosie smiled and shook her head. "You are, you know," she said. "Good at stuff."

. . .

"I'm Goody Morgan," Jilly squealed as we stood in front of the board outside the drama room the Monday after tryouts. Goody Morgan was the female pilgrim with the most lines. Jilly had made her mom drive us to school that morning so we would be the first people to see the cast list. All I could think was, *Thank God.* I didn't think she'd make it through the weekend. She spent most of it rehearsing what she'd say if she got a different part from the lead, things like, "Well, Goody Stanton has more depth to her character" and "Woman Number Three is important because she represents the relationship between the white people and the Native Americans."

"See?" Jilly said, bringing me back to the cast list. "Goody Morgan, dot, dot, dot, dot, dot Jillian Hennessey."

"That's great, Jilly. Can we go now?"

"Wait," she said. "What about you?" Her finger ran down the list of characters, then stopped. "Look. You're an ear of corn."

"What?" I leaned in to get a better look. There it was, printed in a nice field-of-corn yellow from an ink-jet printer. "'I'm all Ears'" Ear of Corn . . . Erin Swift." I groaned. Didn't anyone know this was middle school? Plays using fruits and vegetables as characters went out with the third grade. "I didn't try out for an ear of corn," I said. I hadn't tried out for anything. I mumbled my lines on purpose, sang off-key, tripped over a chair, and missed my cue more than once. I did everything possible not to get a part at all. I only went because Jilly wanted me to.

"You're part of the chorus," Jilly said. "See? Corn, peas, potatoes, yams. All the vegetables are represented."

"I'm not going to be an ear of corn," I hissed in Jilly's ear. "I'm barely over being —"

"There she is!" said a familiar and unwelcome voice behind me. "From puppet to ear of corn. You're moving up in the world, Swift."

I whipped my head around to see Serena standing behind us, smiling her you're-a-loser-and-I'm-not smile. She had been selected to play Goody Stanton in the play, the female with the second most lines.

"Shut up," Jilly and I said at the same time.

"Oooh. Are you going to hit me again? Let's see, that would mean more detention. Or maybe a suspension. Or wait, possibly expell — expellation."

"Expulsion," I said. I couldn't help it. I hated when people used the wrong word.

"You would know," S.W. said. Then she turned to Jilly. "I see you got the lead. Again. Congratulations."

"Thanks, Serena." Jilly pretended not to hear the snot factor in Serena's voice. "See you at rehearsal."

When we were out of earshot, I groaned loudly. "There's no way I'm going to spend the next eight weeks as an ear of corn around her."

"It'll be fun," Jilly said. "Just ignore her."

"That's like telling me to ignore a truck barreling down the highway at me."

"Well, move to the side of the road, Erin. You're going to have to deal with her for the next eight weeks." Jilly fluffed her bangs and tossed her hair. She'd been doing a lot of hair tossing these days. I wondered if she was turning into a horse.

"I don't know if I can do that," I said as we headed toward her locker. Several people called out to us as we passed, and we smiled and waved. Even though they included me in their greetings, I sometimes wondered if they'd notice me if I wasn't with Jilly. After all, this was her territory. Though I came over to this part of the school every morning, it still felt strange. As if I had crossed over the border into a place I didn't quite belong. But I liked being noticed in a good way, not for my feet or being called a puppet. Or now an ear of corn.

An ear of corn. What was I thinking? I planned to spend the next eight weeks as an ear of corn because of Jilly. This seemed to be pushing the limits of friendship, in my opinion.

Jilly took my arm and squeezed it. "Thanks for doing this, Erin. I don't think I could get through it without you."

I sighed. Jilly always seemed to know just what to say when I changed my mind. Giving her a half smile, I tugged at my earlobe. "I'm all ears."

Jilly grinned. "See you after school."

I wondered if anyone else would be an ear of corn for their friend. Somehow, I doubted it.

Monday, September 23

Corn. That's right, folks, I'm playing an ear of corn in the Thanksgiving Harvest play. If Jilly wasn't so excited that I'm doing it with her, I would have turned my kernels in right away. But it was all she could talk about the entire ride home. We'll start script reading next week and full rehearsals in 2 weeks and it just totally bums me out... can't even believe I'm going to spend good after school time singing along with a bunch of vegetables. The things I do for friendship!

But I have to say Jilly has done things for friendship, too... like taking down the Pinocchio posters. She was so funny cuz when I thanked her she smiled and then got a weird look on her face and took off... maybe she's feeling shy about it, which is even weirder.

Today I sat with Mark and Tyler and Rosie at lunch. Rosie had a strange brown drink in her thermos... told me it was chocolate *atole* and asked if I wanted some. Mark was behind her making these "No, don't do it" gestures, but I didn't want to hurt her feelings... tasted a little strange, but I drank most of it cuz it was nice and warm.

Then Mark told me it was basically corn mush... Corn! Don't talk about corn around me! Rosie thinks I'm insane to do the play and I can't explain to her that NO isn't a word I can really use with Jilly.

Things That Are Freaking Me Out 

- I'm corn.
- Serena Poopendena is in the play, 2.

Things That Give Me Hope 

Ms. Moreno told me she was so glad I was part of the Club and, I quote, "We can really use someone like u." Someone like ME.

Question: Who does Ms. Moreno need for the I-Club?

A. A puppet
B. An ear of corn
C. A large-footed mammal
D. None of the above

The correct answer is E for ERIN PENELOPE SWIFT!!!!

Hear that, Serena? Jilly? Ok, that was weird. Why did I write Jilly's name, too? Whatever. MBMS rocks.

chapter 9

Playing With Our Food

Today we had corn — I mean play — practice. I'm now after school four days a week. Monday and Wednesday for the play, Tuesday and Thursday for I-Club. Fridays I get off for good behavior.

I have one line: "I can't HEAR you," and I'm supposed to draw it out. Mrs. Babish, the drama teacher and director of *A Harvest to Remember,* wants me to cup my hand around my ear when I say it. Geez. And we have to learn three songs and sing them as a Vegetable Medley. That was my name for our tasty little group.

The stage sat at one end of the gym, with stairs running up on either side for access. The heavy gray velvet curtains were pulled back against the sides and the skirt across the top of the stage was frayed, the MBMS emblem in the middle starting to fade.

On the way up the steps to the stage, I saw Mr. Foslowski, the now-famous custodian, catcher of illicit smooching.

"Don't even think about using one of my closets," Mr. Foslowski would say to any boy and girl within an arm's length of each other. Then he'd hold up a threatening bottle of Windex and a crumpled paper towel.

Right now he was running a large dust broom across the stage. "Look out, young lady, coming through."

I jumped over the end of the broom and watched him continue across the stage. He looked back at me. "You alone?"

"No. I've got a bunch of vegetables joining me any second."

Mr. Foslowski nodded. "Good. There's safety in numbers." He pushed his glasses up the bridge of his nose. "You look familiar." He peered at me. "I know. You're that girl up on the wall." I cringed as he shook his head. "Those posters were a bear to get down."

"You took them down?" I glanced over at Jilly, who was talking animatedly with the other actors. She smiled and waved at me. I waved back uncertainly.

"Nine of them," Mr. Foslowski said. "They'd used that double-stick spongy tape. If I could've caught them, they would have been the ones scraping it off the walls."

"I'm sorry," I said.

"Why?" he asked. "You didn't put them up there."

"Yeah, but if I hadn't hit her, her friends wouldn't have put them up."

Mr. Foslowski grunted. "Maybe. Maybe not. Kids do some pretty strange things."

I glanced at Jilly again. She looked different somehow, now that I knew she hadn't taken down the posters.

"Okay, people," shouted Mrs. Babish, climbing the side stairs and clapping her hands. "Take your places for Act One, Scene One."

"I'm on," I said to Mr. Foslowski.

"What's your part?" he asked.

I rolled my eyes. "I'm an ear of corn."

"Excellent," he said, as if being an ear of corn was the most normal thing in the world.

. . .

During a break, the Vegetable Medley headed for the water fountain while the rest of the cast rehearsed a scene from Act Two.

"Hey, Swifter than an eagle." I choked on water at the sound of Mark's voice.

"Sack o' Potatoes, what are you doing here?" I stepped away from the fountain. Carla, my locker partner, raised her eyebrows at me. She played a bunch of peas in the Vegetable Medley.

"I'm practicing some coding and I had a question." He glanced across the gym. "Who's that?" He was pointing at the stage. I knew without even looking that he was talking about Jilly.

"She's the lead in the play." *And she acted as if she took down those posters, and she didn't.*

"She's cute."

I grimaced. If you like the blemish-free, perfect hair and teeth look. I was glad the lights were dim except for the stage so he couldn't see my face.

"She seems familiar for some reason. Have I met her before?"

"How should I know?" I snapped, then immediately regretted it. I couldn't show I cared.

Even in the dimness I could see his brow furrow. "Right. Well, can you stop by the lab when you're finished so you can help me?"

"Sure," I said. "That's my job. To help other people." I couldn't even be happy that he needed my help. I watched him go, my stomach twisting and turning.

"He likes her," a voice hissed in my ear. "You didn't think he'd like someone like you."

"Shut up," I said to Serena. My fists clenched beside me, and I turned around to glare at her. "We're friends," I said. "He won't even talk to you."

She tossed her head and walked away as Jilly came over. "Who was that boy?"

"Just a guy from the Intranet Club." My heart was racing. *Please, please don't say you want to meet him.*

"You don't meet on Mondays."

"He's practicing some stuff."

"A real computer geek, huh?"

I smiled, relief flooding through me so fast my knees wobbled. She didn't like nerdy geeks. "You're doing great," I said, steering her away from the Mark topic.

"Thanks, but I feel like I'm never going to learn all these lines." She grabbed my arm. "You need to come over every night this week and help me."

"We just started, Jilly. You'll be fine." I glanced at her. *Why did you act like you took down the posters? Why can't I come out and ask you why you acted like you took down the posters when you didn't?*

"Easy for you to say," Jilly said. "You only have one line."

"And a fine line it is," said Carla, who was so quiet I'd forgotten she was there.

"Why thank you," I said in mock exaggeration. Carla and I giggled. Us veggies had to stick together. Jilly rolled her eyes while I finished the drink Mark had interrupted.

While I slurped, Jilly blabbed about how important her role was and how the entire cast was counting on her. I found myself saying, "Blah, blah, blah," in my mind as she talked. I stopped drinking and took a breath, letting the water run while I watched it arch gracefully in the air before circling down the small drain. Why couldn't I ever seem to get as much in my mouth as I wanted? I always felt like I was gulping at it like a fish in a bowl. I wondered if they could design the fountain differently so we didn't waste so much water when we got a drink. Or —

"Erin?" Someone tapped on my shoulder. "Erin, are you listening to me?"

I turned to look at Jilly, who was frowning at me.

"Yes," I said, though I had no idea what she had just said. I glanced at Carla, who just smiled at me. I could tell she was sort of in awe of Jilly.

"Can I get a drink now?" asked Jilly. "My throat is dry from all that talking."

I stepped away from the water fountain. "I'm done."

Jilly tossed her hair over her shoulder and held it back with one hand, turning on the fountain with the other. She was the only person I knew who could drink from a drinking fountain without slurping.

"So, how many lines do you have?" Carla asked Jilly.

"Forty-seven." Jilly looked toward the stage. "I think they're starting again. I'll meet you after rehearsal." She took off across the floor before I could respond.

"I can't hear you," I said softly to the empty air.

Carla's eyes were on me but mine were on Jilly. She stood in the middle of the stage, so sure of herself, smiling and nodding at Mrs. Babish. Watching her, I suddenly felt like there was a whole world separating us, not just half a gymnasium.

"Hey, Erin," said Carla, startling me. "I think we're on."

We took our places as Mr. Trubey, the music teacher, strode across the gymnasium toward the stage. He took the steps two at a time and seated himself at the piano.

"Okay," he said, lightly fingering the keys. "Let's walk through the opening piece." He looked over at us. "Corn? Lend me your ear. Squash? Let's be careful where we sit. Peas? Thank you."

I rolled my eyes at Carla who rolled hers back, but we couldn't help smiling at his puns.

"Okay, people," Mr. Trubey said, raising his hands. "Let's make it organic."

. . .

When I got home, Chris was doing his homework in front of the television.

"How many times do I have to tell you —" Mom said before Chris cut her off.

"Okay, okay." He clicked off the TV, staring at the blank screen.

"Want to shoot some hoops after you finish?" I asked him as Mom headed for the kitchen. I couldn't believe he was still mad at me about the Hitting Serena–Amanda thing.

Chris's eyes moved slowly from the blank TV screen to me, then back again.

"I'll take that as a maybe," I said, and headed out to the driveway. Soon I was dribbling and shooting, working my way around the key, a wavy half-circle we'd painted on the cement to mark the three-second lane and foul line. As I put up a three-pointer, Chris appeared below the basket and caught the ball as it swished through.

"And the crowd goes wild," I said, waving my hands in the air as I made crowd noises. Chris whizzed the ball at me and if I hadn't been so quick, the pass might have knocked me off my feet. I stifled an "umph," feeling as if the ball had left a crater in my stomach. I recovered, planted my feet, and shot again. It bounced off the rim. He passed it again. I shot again. This time it bounced off the backboard and off to the side. He scrambled for it.

"You're not following through," he said before passing me the ball.

"Okay. Thanks." I shot again, this time making sure my right hand continued in a forward motion after the ball. The ball hit the backboard and dropped into the basket.

"Right," Chris said, passing it to me.

I passed it back. "Your turn."

Chris twisted from his place beneath the basket, leaped up, and sank the ball neatly.

"Two points," I said, smiling. He grunted. "Look, Chris. I'm sorry I hit Serena and ruined your chances with Amanda. I had no idea."

And even if I had, I'm not sure it would have stopped me from hitting Serena when she called me a puppet.

Chris shrugged. "You know what? It's not a big deal. I just had the most beautiful girl on the entire campus actually noticing my existence when *wham!* You give her sister a right hook."

"Actually, it was a straight-on punch," I said. "But that doesn't matter. I'm just sorry it happened." I crossed my arms. "And it would have been nice if you cared a little bit about what happened to me."

"She called you a stupid word. Who cares? Why did you get so bent about it?" He dribbled back and swished a basket from the sidewalk. "Unless you thought it was true."

"It isn't!" I shouted, stealing the ball from him and dribbling it back.

"Then why'd you hit her?"

"She deserved it," I said, echoing Rosie. "You don't know what she's like."

Chris shrugged, raising his arm to easily block my shot.

"Just don't do any more stupid things that might affect my life, Erin." He made his layup, then headed toward the porch, letting the ball bounce toward me.

I made a face. "Like I'm going to know that in advance."

 **Thursday, October 10**

Things That Bum Me Out 

- Chris is still mad. I miss having a brother...even though he's in high school and acts like he hates me a lot of the time, sometimes we shoot hoops or watch a movie together or something...really glad he came out, but then it ended up that he just wanted to get mad at me some more. (Sigh)

- Jilly didn't take down the posters and she acted like she did—didn't deny it...and she always corrects me when I call play practice "practice." "It's a REHEARSAL," she says, as if a word is going to change the fact that I will get up in front of 100s of people as a singing ear of corn.

- Jilly talks A LOT...all of it about herself...didn't realize how much she does this. She hasn't once asked me what I thought of playing an ear of corn...had to tell her I had 1 line and she didn't even comment, like how could I even bring that up when her part was so much bigger and harder. Sheesh. Give me a break.

When we finished practice—I mean rehearsal—Carla said how great Jilly was and said she wished she was like her. I wanted to tell her "No, you don't" and I don't know why. I always wanted to be like Jilly, 2...wanted her confidence, the way she could get boys to look at her, the way she knew how to talk to them without looking like an idiot...guess I still want those things but don't really want to be like Jilly. I want to be like me, only more confident and with smaller feet.

Things That Give Me Hope 

- Jilly wouldn't come to the lab with me after rehearsal. "I might get infected with nerd-itis," she said...told me to meet her at her locker after I talked to Mark. I was SO SO glad but I pretended to be disappointed.

Operation Scope Out 

Close call with Jilly and Mark today...got to take action ASAP. Tomorrow I'm going to scope Mark out in secret...make sure we accidentally-on-purpose bump into each other and walk to class again. For the 2nd time since school started, I'm glad Jilly isn't on my track cuz she'd find a way to get Mark. But she doesn't even know he exists. He's mine, all mine (evil laugh here).

chapter 10

Target Practice

8:25 A.M. Target (aka Mark "Cute Boy" Sacks) stepped off his bus. He looked our way, and I turned sideways so he couldn't see Jilly. I stood on tiptoe to shield her head from sight. When she asked me what I was doing, I told her I had a cramp in both feet, then quickly asked her to repeat her lines to me even though I'd heard them so many times *I* could play Goody Morgan. She began reciting, and I got her inside without her seeing him or him seeing her.

8:35 A.M. Target entered the building wearing baggy jeans and a Nike T-shirt. Hair still over one eye, looking very cute. Target appeared to be heading this way so I turned quickly, stumbling over my Chucks. Real swift, Swift. I glanced back, my eyes on the clock so Target would not think I was looking at him. Target was stopped by an unidentified boy in a blue shirt. Unidentified pointed. My eyes followed his finger. It was some kind of poster. Oh, no. Tell me it wasn't another of those posters, bigger and better than the ones that were up that first week.

8:37 A.M. "Hey, Swift!" Mayday! Mayday! Target was talking to me. I'd blown my cover. Well, I really didn't have a cover, but if I had one, I would have totally blown it. Was he going to say something about the poster? I wanted to run but was afraid I'd trip so I decided to stand tough. I dug around in my locker, ready to do battle if he dared make a joke about puppets.

8:40 A.M. Target arrived at my locker with two friends. I ended all Scope Out procedures right then. I can't scope at close range.

"Did you see that poster?" he asked.

I shook my head quickly. "I don't want to hear about it."

"Oh, it isn't —"

I held up my hand.

"Okay," he said. "Whatever. But this Saturday, Swift. The YMCA. Be there or be a loser." His friends looked me up and down. They probably already thought I was one.

"What?"

"Basketball," he said. "Remember when the four of us played? You said you could kill me one-on-one. It's time to prove it."

"Prove it?" We'd been kidding around about who was better, but I never thought he'd really want to play.

"He's not as good as he says," one of the boys said.

"Yeah," said Mark. "I'm better."

I laughed. "I've seen you. I'll be there. Get ready to be dominated."

The boys laughed and I felt better. No one seemed to think I was a loser.

"Hey, there's another one," Mark said as we started down the hall. He was pointing at one of the walls. I swung around, ready to yank down my oversize face if I had to.

But it wasn't a picture of me.

THANKSGIVING PLAY!

Mark your calendars for the Molly Brown Middle School play

A Harvest to Remember

Tuesday, November 26, 7:30 P.M., in the gymnasium

"Look, Corny," said Mark. "You're famous again."

Before I could respond, his eyes grew wide. "Here comes the principal."

I whirled around. Yikes. She was coming right at me.

"Erin Swift! Just the girl I wanted to see."

I looked up at her. "I haven't hit anyone else, Mrs. Porter. I promise."

"Oh, I know that, Erin. Heavens." She smiled. "I just wanted to say I'm glad to see you're getting involved in the school. I understand you're in the Thanksgiving play" — she paused to point to the poster — "and Ms. Moreno tells me you're in the Intranet Club, too. The best way to stay out of trouble is to get involved."

I kept my eyes on her, ignoring Mark, who was making marionette gestures behind her back, just inside my field of vision. "Yes, well, I thought so, too."

"Excellent," Mrs. Porter said. "And how are your puppets?"

I glanced at Mark, who rolled his eyes. "Uh, they're fine, Mrs. Porter," I said. "Just fine."

Mark busted out laughing when she was gone. "Good answer," he said. "She's so weird."

"Yeah," I said, laughing along with him. I didn't care how weird she was. She'd just helped Mark and me have a good laugh together.

• • •

"Ready to rumble?" Mark and I stood facing each other on the basketball court at the YMCA Saturday afternoon. My suspicious mind wondered if this was all a way to find out about Jilly. He knew I knew her from the play. Maybe he wanted more information. But he wouldn't do that. Would he? Nah.

Okay, I felt better about that. But the minute I had convinced myself this wasn't about Jilly, I started stressing about getting together with him. True, I got to be with the boy of my dreams. BUT, I'd be playing a sport with him. This meant I'd be sweating, breathing heavily, and very possibly farting around him. This last one had me VERY paranoid, so I'd made extra sure not to eat anything yesterday or today that might be even remotely related to a bean.

So here I was, facing Mark, who was between me and the basket at the Y, praying I wouldn't sweat, burp, fart, or do anything stupid. I looked down at my Chucks. Both were tied in triple knots. Mark's eyes followed mine down.

"They give me balance," I said, before he could say anything about my feet. "I can out-balance anyone."

"Huh?"

"My feet. You were going to say something, weren't you?"

"No. Actually I was going to ask you where you got your Chuck Taylors. My dad likes canvas shoes and can't always find them."

I narrowed my eyes. Was he saying my feet were the same size as his dad's? I decided to give him the benefit of the doubt. "Foot Locker."

"Thanks. I'll tell him." Then he got a glint in his eye. "Maybe he could try yours on first."

Wham! I knocked the ball out of his hands and ducked around him, dribbling to the basket and making an easy layup — all before he knew he held nothing but air. He looked down, then turned around. "Hey, that was cheating!"

"No way!" I replied. "You just weren't ready. Two-zero."

"I'm supposed to pass to you first to check the ball."

"Is that with or without a foot insult?"

Mark smiled. "Sorry. I couldn't resist. Especially because you were expecting me to say something." He cocked his head. God, he was cute. "I thought you could take it."

I shook off the Cute Spell. "I can take it," I said evenly. "Can you take this?" I shoved the ball at him and he caught it in the chest. I heard an "umph" as his hands wrapped around it.

"Nice pass," he said, dribbling out past the top of the key before coming back. "You know you're lucky, don't you? Those feet mean you're going to be tall."

"So I hear," I said, blocking his shot and retrieving the ball. I dribbled back up to the key, feinting left and going right to avoid his reaching hand. "I guess that'll be good if I play in the WNBA." I wondered if he liked tall girls. Some boys — the ones that were totally lame — didn't. What if all boys were lame and no one ever wanted to go out with me? I missed my shot and Mark got the rebound.

Between games we talked a little more. I found myself telling him about Chris.

"Guys are weird when they like a girl," Mark said, then blushed. "Not that I've liked that many, but you know."

No, I don't know! I wanted to shout. *Tell me all about it.* But I was afraid he might start telling me about Jilly or maybe some other girl I didn't even know, and I couldn't stand that.

"I just wish he'd stop being mad," I said. "Ever since he got into high school, he treats me like I'm this little immature kid or something."

Mark smiled. "Compared to sixteen, we are immature."

"Speak for yourself," I said, taking a shot from the top of the key. *Swish.*

"At least you don't have a sister who thinks you're cute like a puppy dog and introduces you to all her college friends like you're her pet." Mark made a face. "She thinks she's this big adult and I'm a little kid she needs to take care of."

"Ugh." I wasn't sure which was worse.

We kept playing, sharing tidbits of information with each other. Then Mark went for a layup. I jumped to block it, but my arm got tangled in his. We dropped down together in a heap and when we looked at each other, our faces were super close. I was looking right into his eyes, our noses practically touching, his lips about two inches from mine. My heart pounded crazily in my chest and I held my breath. Could this be it?

Our eyes held for a moment and then Mark untangled his arm and rolled away, bouncing to his feet.

"Foul," he said. "I get two shots."

"No way!" I scrambled to get up, trying to hide my face, which was getting warmer by the second. I wiped my hands on my shorts and squared my shoulders. He could never know I thought we were about to kiss. Never. "I didn't touch you on the way up."

"Foul," he said again, grinning.

"Cheater," I muttered. But I stood on the foul lane, ready for the rebound. Neither of us said anything about being face-to-face, but I couldn't stop thinking about it. He beat me easily, 20 to 15. In the end, he won three games and I won two.

"Okay," Mark said. "Where will I kick your butt next? Baseball field? Football?"

"The soccer field," I said. "Where else?"

"No way," Mark said. "You'd kick my butt."

"I know." I picked up my basketball as we headed across the gym toward the water fountains. Placing it on top of my index finger, I spun it, smacking it to keep it going.

"You're the first girl I've ever seen do that," Mark said. He started spinning his, and pretty soon we had dueling spinning basketballs.

"My brother taught me," I said, glancing at the clock. "We can time ourselves. Best two out of three?"

"You're on," Mark said.

Saturday, October 12

Things That Make Me Think Mark Is My Friend

- He talks to me 1st. I'm not always going up to him.
- He plays basketball with me.
- He makes fun of me in a good way.

Things That Make Me Think Mark Is Using Me

- Boys have used me B4 to get to Jilly.
- Not so long ago, I was a puppet.
- Not so long ago, Mark saw me almost pull a table down on top of myself.
- Not so long ago, Mark gawked at my best friend at play practice.

I can't help it. I keep thinking he's trying to get to Jilly. I've never had a friend that's a boy B4, just boys I play sports with, not talk to about stuff.

Today I went really crazy. Mark said he wanted to ask me something and suddenly I was convinced that there was a hidden camera nearby and any minute some hyper announcer with a banana-wide smile would jump out of 1 of the Y restrooms and shout, "Erin P. Swift, You Fell for It!" I would find out that I was the subject of a new TV show where losers were approached by people who would never talk to them in their wildest dreams and act like they were friends. Just when the Losers were about to fall down and kiss the feet of the person who was talking to them, the announcer would break their cover and shout, "You Fell for It!"

I could see it now, like the opening of the show was being played out in front of me.

"Good afternoon, ladies and gentlemen, and welcome to 'You Fell for It,' where we track gullible losers with a hidden camera, watching them make fools of themselves as they believe someone cool would actually talk to them! Today's unsuspecting contestant is Miss Erin P. Swift, also known as Pinocchio, who will be approached by Cute Boy himself, Mark Sacks!" Applause, applause, applause as they project a 6-foot copy of the Erin-Pinoccho-Ped picture up on the screen behind the announcer. Then they cut to a shot of the YMCA hallway, where an unsuspecting Erin Swift (that's me) is walking down the hall with the Cool Person (Mark Sacks). He's there in all his cuteness, lulling her with that 1-eyed gaze, making her swoon, and just B4 she drops to her knees, ready to kiss his feet—

But then he just wanted to know my opinion on using software that creates web pages or just using HTML.

I think I'm being paranoid. I hope I am. PLEASE let it just be paranoia.

I may or may not kiss his feet, it would depend on whether they were clean or not... wouldn't mind kissing his lips... never kissed a boy I liked B4, only boys I didn't like when we played spin the bottle. 1 guy stuffed his tongue down my throat like he was trying to lick my tonsils...GROSS OUT. But Mark and I were THIS close to kissing on the basketball court. I know we were...and it would not have been disgusting.

I hope we get another chance.

In the meantime, I think I'll practice kissing my pillow. 

chapter 11

Erin Swift, Scout

"So who did you play basketball with yesterday?"

We were lying across Jilly's bed, flipping through her latest issue of *CosmoGIRL!* while we waited for her mom to get off the phone so she could take us to the mall. Jilly wanted (she said "needed") a new shirt. More competition with that blonde.

I squinted at the page in front of me, pretending not to hear.

"Was it Rosie?"

"Huh?" I closed the magazine. Looking at those glossy girls made me feel like a total loser. I pulled out my copy of *Sports Illustrated* and opened it up.

"Did you play basketball with Rosie on Saturday? I called your house and your dad said you'd gone to play basketball with a friend." She pulled the magazine out from under my nose. "Who's your friend? I hope it wasn't Rosie."

It almost sounded as if Jilly was a wee bit jealous. But she'd already made a ton of friends at MBMS, and if I'd made only one, she couldn't be mad about that.

"No, it wasn't Rosie. Just . . . someone I met at school."

"Do I know her? Did she go to Jordan last year?"

I frowned. Of course she assumed it was a girl. But I wasn't going to tell her about Mark.

"Okay, girls! I'm ready." Mrs. Hennessey stood in the doorway, smiling. "Sorry about that but now we've got to hustle. My hair appointment is in twenty minutes."

"I want to get my hair done for the Spring Dance," Jilly said, sliding off the bed. "We should go all out."

The Spring Dance was almost five months away, but that didn't stop Jilly from planning. I was grateful for the change of subject, even though I knew I wouldn't be going "all out." I wouldn't be going at all.

"Definitely," I said.

Jilly sighed. "I hope someone asks me."

"Of course someone will ask you," I said, smacking her arm. "Are you crazy?"

When we got to the mall, Mrs. Hennessey gave us strict instructions to meet her back at the hair salon in an hour. "No dawdling."

Jilly saluted and we both laughed as we hurried across to PacSun. She rummaged through the jeans racks, pulling out pair after pair to try on.

"Do you even have any money?" I asked.

"Just enough for two smoothies," she said. "But I'll put these on my Christmas list. Dad's leaving for New York Thursday so I should have them by Sunday." Jilly's dad traveled a lot so she would sometimes leave a magazine open with something circled, or a list lying around with things she wanted. The next time he got home, he usually had a "surprise" for her.

As she turned a carousel of blouses, she gasped. "It's that boy from the bus," she said, ducking down to the floor. I turned to look. It was the boy who had said, "Jillian-not-Geppetto" on the second day of school.

"Why are you down there?"

She yanked me down next to her. "I don't want him to see me."

"Why not?"

“He might think we’re following him. That would be lame.”

“Jilly, we’re inside a store. He’s in the middle of the mall by a fountain. How could we be following him?”

“He might think we’re spying. You know, ducking into stores as we go.” She scooted under the rack and peered out between two blouses.

And I thought I had a wild imagination. “He’s not even looking this way.”

Jilly leaped up, knocking three blouses to the floor. “Don’t look at him,” she said. “Just act natural.”

I wasn’t really looking at him and I was acting natural, but I turned my head anyway. Picking up the shirts Jilly had knocked down, I watched while she moved to another rack. I could see her out of my peripheral vision. “You’re looking at him.”

“That’s because he’s not looking this way now.” She whipped her head toward me. “Okay, now he is.” She bent to tie her shoe, which was already tied. “Is he still looking at me?”

“Are you saying it’s okay for me to look at him?”

“Yes! Yes!”

“Why can I look at him now but I couldn’t look at him before?”

Jilly groaned in exasperation. “Because before we were both standing and it would have been obvious, but now you’re already facing that way and I’m down here so it’s natural that you would look over that way.”

“Oh.” This boy surveillance thing was pretty complicated.

“Well?”

“He’s not looking at you. He’s eating a pretzel and jabbing his friend with a straw.” I could see him better now. I frowned at Jilly. “So do you want him to see you or not?”

“I want him to see me, but I don’t want him to think that I saw him first because then it’ll look like I’m after him when I’m not. He’s really after me.”

"Oh."

She was still on the floor, retying her other shoe now. I glanced back out the window.

"He's leaving," I said.

"He's leaving?" Jilly bounced up and ran to the window. "Follow him."

"What?"

"Just go out and see which store he goes in."

"I thought you just said you didn't want him to think we're following him. That it would be lame."

"It would be lame if *I* followed him, not if *you* followed him."

I furrowed my brow. "Why not?"

"Erin, he's getting away. Please!" She practically shoved me toward the door.

"Geez, Jilly. All right. All right." I shrugged her hands off my back. Turning on my heel to face her, I saluted. "Erin Swift reporting for duty."

Jilly rolled her eyes, but I could tell she was fighting a smile. "Just go already."

I turned back toward the door and performed an exaggerated march.

"Don't do that when you get out there," Jilly said.

I saluted again and returned to my normal walk as I stepped out of the store. I took a few steps in the direction of Bus Boy and his pal. Bus Boy kept walking, then stopped in front of a music store. He quickly downed his drink and scarfed down his pretzel, leaving the cup on the floor outside the store. Litterbug. Minus two points.

As he and his friend entered the store, he paused. Swiveling his head, he looked right at me. I was so startled, I just stared. He grinned and waved at me. I waved back. I didn't know what else to do. Once he was safely inside the store, I ran back to Jilly.

"Did you just wave at him?" Jilly turned from the window, where she had had her nose pressed against the glass.

"He waved first," I protested. "I didn't know what else to do."

"I can't believe you waved at him," Jilly said, shaking her head. "You totally blew our cover."

"I only blew my cover," I said. "Yours is still safe."

I looked at some shirts and a jacket while Jilly made out her Christmas list. We walked over to another store (after I snuck ahead to make sure Bus Boy was nowhere in sight), and Jilly added to her list.

"I was going to look at some CDs but we can't go anywhere near that music store now," Jilly said. We sat at a table near Juice Express, sipping a couple of smoothies. "Hey, I think that's Brian Johnson." Jilly dropped her head under the table.

"Who?"

"Brian Johnson," Jilly said, her voice muffled by the table top. "He's in my homeroom. Isn't he cute?"

"The one in the blue shirt and earring?"

Jilly popped up, then popped back down. "Yeah."

"Yes. He is. Cuter than Bus Boy."

"Who?"

"The boy we were spying on earlier. Bus Boy. The one on our bus."

"Oh, right. I think he's an eighth grader." She paused. "Where's Brian?"

I took a sip of my smoothie, making her wait as I hatched my diabolical plan. "You can come out now. He just went into Structure."

Jilly sat up. Brian stood only a few yards from our table.

"Jillian!" He waved at her and she waved back, smoothing her hair, which stuck out at odd ends because she had been practically upside-down under the table.

"I hate you," she whispered out of the corner of her mouth as she smiled at Brian.

“No, you don’t,” I said. She looked at me and laughed.

“You’re right,” she said. “You may be a sneak, but you’re a good friend. Thanks for playing spy.”

“You’re welcome,” I said. “Thanks for the smoothie.” We drank in silence for a while. “I think Brian likes you.”

“Umm,” Jilly said, her chin in her hand as she leaned her elbow on the table.

“If he still likes you in the spring, I bet he asks you to the dance. I bet you’ll have so many guys asking you, you’ll have to put their names in a hat and draw one out.”

Jilly laughed. “I wish.”

I didn’t say anything else. But I did wonder what it would be like to have someone like me. I didn’t need a whole hatful of guys. Just one.

chapter 12

Ouch

"You'd never know you were a puppet, except from back here." Mark was walking slightly behind me as we headed for the computer lab. We'd been hard at it for a few weeks now, first developing the Intranet and then the content. The idea that everything we wrote and created would be seen by every kid at MBMS was starting to freak us all out. We realized how important everything we did was. Mark and I talked practically nonstop about web pages and other stuff, in addition to having a few pickup games of basketball in the gym with some other kids to give our brains a break.

"I can see where the strings come out." Mark tapped me lightly on the back, sending a shiver through me. I shook my head, but I couldn't help smiling. Only Mark Sacks could say something like that and have it send my heart soaring. It was so great to be friends with him that it was almost okay that he didn't like me more than a friend. Almost.

"You know you're the only one who still talks about the PI," I said. "When are you going to get over it?"

Mark smiled and shrugged. "It's fun to tease you." He flipped his bangs back, and I raised my eyebrows in mock surprise.

"You *do* have another eye."

"Yeah, I let it out every once in a while to stretch."

I laughed as we stepped into the lab.

"Erin, check this out." Rosie waved me over.

"That looks great," I said, leaning over her shoulder. "I like that font."

"Hey, Erin, are you all ears?" I glanced over at Steve, who was in Mark's group. He was grinning and tugging at his ears. Then he pointed to his screen and read aloud, "Molly Brown Middle School was proud to present *A Harvest to Remember,* starring blah, blah, blah, and our own Erin Swift as . . ." He swiveled around in his chair. "Drumroll, please . . . an ear of corn!"

"Ha, ha, ha," I said, shaking my head. I didn't know why they even had to put it on the Intranet since it would be over before we went live. But Ms. Moreno didn't want to leave any events out. "I tried out as a favor to a friend and got stuck in the vegetable chorus, okay?"

Steve whirled back around in his chair, chuckling to himself. A few titters ping-ponged around the rest of the room, but it all seemed good-natured. Serena sneered but I ignored her. I was in my element now. Her meanness couldn't penetrate my webmaster shield.

Ms. Moreno smiled at me. "I like to see that mix of the arts and science."

"Thanks," I said as I headed to my group.

Tyler leaned over as I sat down at my computer. "I think you'll make a great ear of corn." His hair gel almost made me gag but I held it back and scowled instead.

"I'm serious," he protested. He did look like he meant it.

"Thanks," I said. "I think."

He smiled and looked back at his monitor.

We worked hard for the next two and a half hours, taking only a quick snack break at the vending machines. When 5:30 rolled around, I logged off and scrambled out the door. I had exactly thirty minutes to get home and then go over to Jilly's to help her with her lines.

• • •

"Tell them they are welcome. Everyone is welcome. They have given us much, taught us much, and we are —"

"They have given us so much and taught us even more —" I interrupted.

"Darn it," said Jilly, slapping her thigh. "That 'much, much' speech comes later." She strode over to her starting place and began walking toward the center of the room. "Tell them they are welcome. Everyone is welcome. They have given us so much and taught us even more. I will speak with your father about a welcoming party."

I clapped loudly and Jilly grinned before collapsing on the floor with the back of one hand thrown over her forehead in an exaggerated gesture.

I reached down and she gave me five.

"Thanks, Erin," she said. "You're a lifesaver."

• • •

When I got back from Jilly's, Chris was lounging on the couch, flipping through the channels. I dropped into a chair next to him.

"Mom said you would take me to the library before it closed."

Chris ignored me, clicked again, and came to rest on ESPN.

I glanced at the clock on the wall. "We've got forty-five minutes. They're holding the book at the counter so I'll be fast."

He blinked and folded his arms over his chest, the clicker peeking out from under one elbow. I leaned over and pressed the MUTE button.

"I thought by the time you were sixteen you didn't do stuff like the ST." Neither of us had used the Silent Treatment on each other in years.

Chris clicked the MUTE off and the room filled with the roar of an engine from the next commercial. He watched the rest of the commercial, then groaned and turned it off.

"Let's go." He strode across the room, grabbed the car keys off the hook, and stalked out the door without his jacket.

"Wait up!" I called, hurrying after him. "Mom, Chris is taking me to the library!"

"Okay, honey."

I hoped he was. I was afraid he might leave me, even though the whole point of him driving was to take me to the library. I made sure my library card was in my pocket and scurried out to the garage.

. . .

Chris pulled into a parking space that faced the street. Turning off the ignition, he tapped his fingers impatiently on the wheel. "Hurry up."

"You're not coming in?"

He shook his head.

I ran inside and was back in a few minutes, my book clutched in my hand. When I opened the door, I noticed the car's dome light didn't go on. "Hey, I think the light's —"

Chris grabbed my wrist and pulled me inside. "Close the door! Quick!"

I ducked, barely missing the door frame as I fell into my seat and slammed the door. I stared at him in the darkness.

"What's up?"

"Get down." Chris was slumped way down in his seat. I looked through the windows, trying to figure out what we were hiding from. "Stop looking around and get down," he hissed, grabbing my arm again. I slid down in the seat, having a strange sense of déjà vu. I rearranged my knees under the dash and held my breath, even though I didn't need to. No one could possibly hear me breathing through a closed door. Chris was staring out the window, his hands gripping the steering wheel. Between two of his fingers dangled the basketball key chain I had given him when he was eleven and I was seven. He usually wore it in a belt loop with no keys on it and had it with him for every basketball game he played. He said it was good luck.

"There she is," Chris whispered to himself, jolting my eyes from the silver basketball to his face. I dared raise my head two inches so I could see out. A girl stood under the streetlight at the corner. She was magazine-cover beautiful, with long blond hair that curled softly at the ends. Her sweater showed off a very nice set of boobolas and she wore tight black jeans and stylish boots.

Amanda Worthington. It had to be. I shook my head slightly, wondering how I was once again spying on someone's love interest. I sighed. Always the spy, never the spy-ee.

Letting out my breath, I glanced over at Chris. Even in the dim light, I could see his longing. Is that how I looked when I looked at Mark? Suddenly I felt guilty, as if I was reading Chris's journal or listening in on a private conversation. I turned my eyes back to Amanda. She was looking over her shoulder, smiling and tapping her foot. Seconds later a boy appeared at her side, throwing his arm casually across her shoulders as they walked down the sidewalk. I sucked in my breath and sank way down in my seat, counting to five before looking over the dashboard. They were just past our car. Amanda leaned toward the boy and kissed him right on the mouth. One Mississippi, two Mississippi, three Mississippi, four Mississippi, five Mississippi, six Mississippi. She pulled back slowly. Wow. That was one long kiss. The boy brushed her hair away from her face, and they continued down the sidewalk before turning the corner and disappearing.

I didn't dare look at Chris. I slouched there, clutching my book in my lap, trying not to breathe.

"Crap," Chris swore under his breath. He tossed the key chain over his shoulder and I heard it hit the backseat. Jamming the keys in the ignition, he started the car and backed quickly out of the parking space. I sat up and clicked my seat belt into place, gripping the door handle as Chris drove madly down the street, his jaw clenched as he stared out the windshield.

But I knew he wasn't seeing the road. I knew he was seeing that kiss, playing it over and over in his mind. And I knew that no matter how fast he drove, he couldn't get away from it.

Saturday, October 26

So, things have been weird and I haven't felt like writing for a while. I've never, ever felt sorry for my brother in my entire life. He's always been better, smarter, and funnier than me. But Thurs. night outside the library, I felt so sorry for him I thought I would cry. And I might have, except I was so afraid we were going to crash on the way home that I couldn't. He was SO mad. He really likes Amanda Worthington and he saw her kissing this boy. What if I saw Mark kissing someone? I would DIE... absolutely DIE.

So, I'm bumming about him but then I had this great day with Rosie and Mark. We went with Ms. Moreno to the university to hook up with some Intranet people... got some ideas for our own Intranet. Way fun... met 2 of the people who will be leading a web camp this summer, so that was really cool. At lunch we laughed so hard that Rosie's pop sprayed out her nose. It went all over her fries, so I shared mine with her. Hilarious... but then I kind of felt guilty cuz I was having so much fun without Jilly... as if she's never done stuff without me. Geez.

Mark looked unbelievably cute today (when does he not?). The bangs over the eye are to die for... we teased each other about basketball. He told Rosie I was "really good for a girl." We both smacked him. He laughed... said Rosie hates when he says that... she said that's why he says it, then she hits him. The coolest thing of all was she said I was now part of the routine. I couldn't believe it. I'm PART OF THE ROUTINE. Is that great or what???

I tried really hard not to stare at Mark. I couldn't help wondering what it would be like to kiss him for 6 Mississippis.

Wonder if my pillow-kissing practice will pay off in a real kissing situation . . . wonder if I'll ever know.

chapter 13

Howlingween

Now that we're in seventh grade, Halloween is about parties, not trick-or-treating. Jilly and I went to an after-school costume party at the rec center on Halloween day. Whoever was in charge of decorating must have had kids under the age of five because they'd hung lame orange and black paper streamers across the ceiling, tacked cardboard witches and pumpkins to the walls, and left a cauldron of wispy dry ice in the corner.

But Jilly didn't seem to mind. She waved to Frankenstein's monster across the floor, then started dancing with some of her C Track friends when a good song came on. The DJ was dressed like a pirate, looking extra scruffy in the flash of strobe lights. He shouted encouragement whenever someone ventured onto the dance floor, dissing the boys who stood in clumps of two or three on the other side of the room.

"Come on, Erin!" Jilly tugged at my arm but I shook my head. These peds weren't made for dancing and there was no way I was going out there. Jilly waved at me and joined her friends, shimmying and shaking to the beat.

I glanced around, trying to spot someone, *anyone,* I might know. I knew there were a lot of kids from MBMS, but they were hard to recognize in their costumes.

Jilly finally came off the dance floor and joined me. We stood off to the side as she caught her breath.

"Boo!" said a voice behind me, and I turned to see an ugly beast, its mouth dripping with blood pumped through a thin tube.

"Gross," Jilly said, shaking her head. She'd dressed up as a pop star, complete with diamond-studded belly button, fake boobs, and tons of makeup. She looked about eighteen and boys were definitely giving her the eye.

"I'm Mark," said the Beast, holding out a furry paw.

"Sacks?" I asked, grabbing his arm. "Sack o' Potatoes, is that you in there?" I turned my head, nearly slicing Jilly's cheek with one of my Pippy Longstocking hair wires.

"Erin! Watch it!" Jilly ducked and brushed a hand across her Pop Star Blush #3.

"It's me," Mark answered, but his head was turned toward Jilly. Why, oh why didn't I dress up like a sexy rock star? Well, maybe because I'd rather have a virus attack my hard drive than have people staring at various parts of my body the way they were staring at Jilly. Besides, how many sexy rock stars have feet the size of a small guitar? Answer: none. So I stood there all stiff and awkward, looking at Mark looking at Jilly.

"Pippi!" Rosie pounced at me, baring her vampire fangs as she flung back her high-collared cape. She had painted her face white, with black circles around her eyes. "Watch," she said, leaning toward me. She clenched her teeth. Blood oozed over her fangs and down her chin.

"Gross!" Jilly scrunched up her nose.

"What's with the two of you and dripping blood?" I asked, laughing.

"Isn't it great?" Rosie said. "You just bite into these things and it looks like blood." She held out a handful of dark capsules.

"Don't get too close," Jilly said. "They'll stain my costume." She hitched up her breasts, and Mark the Beast was mesmerized.

"Quit drooling and get us a drink." Rosie smacked Mark's arm.

"In a minute," Mark said, still staring at Jilly. He pretended to adjust his mask, but I could see his eyes riveted through the eyeholes.

Time to take action.

"So, great costume," I said, tugging his furry arm. "Let me see that blood thing." I moved my hand in front of his eyes, pretending I couldn't find the tube. This seemed to break his trance.

"Huh?" Mark asked. "Uh, yeah. Pretty cool, huh?"

"Hey, Erin. Great costume."

I cocked my head at an alien who had appeared before us.

"It's me, Tyler."

"Tyler? Wow. It's cool how that lights up." I pointed to his mask, but I was watching Mark out of the corner of my eye. He was back to watching Jilly, who was watching some people dancing.

"Yeah," Tyler said. "But the batteries keep bumping against my head. The thing holding them up broke off." There was a shout and he looked over his shoulder. "Oops. It's my turn at the race car game. See you later."

An elbow dug into my ribs. Rosie's lips brushed my ear. "He likes you," she whispered.

"What?" I said, practically choking on my gum. "No way."

"He does," Rosie said. "Can't you tell?"

"No," I said. No boy had ever liked me. How in the world was I supposed to "tell"?

"What are you two talking about?" Jilly asked.

"Computer stuff," I said. Jilly rolled her eyes. Then she looked at Tyler, who was huddled over a video game.

"He's a little goofy," Mark said to Jilly. There was a howl across the room and Mark lifted his head. "Gotta run, girls. The brothers are calling." With a loud howl back, Mark was gone.

"And he's not?" Jilly asked no one in particular. She shook her head. "We need high school boys, Erin." I noticed she wasn't including Rosie in the conversation.

"High school boys?" I said. "Don't they shave and have underarm hair?" I looked at Rosie, but she had already backed away into the crowd.

"Well, at least they aren't howling at their friends like they're in some sort of wolf clan."

My heart soared. "I think it's called a pack," I said to distract her even further.

"What?"

"A group of wolves," I said. "It's called a pack."

"Oh, Erin. Who cares? The point is seventh-grade boys are immature. Come on, let's go over by the punch bowl. Elvis has been staring at me all afternoon. I think he's an eighth grader."

• • •

I answered the door for trick-or-treaters that night while Mom and Dad ate Chinese food in the kitchen. Chris had gone out with some of his friends to a party. I fell asleep in front of the TV at nine and my dad got me off to bed. I woke up suddenly at 12:14, just as a car door slammed outside. Slipping out of bed, I tiptoed across my room and peered out the window.

Chris was standing next to his friend's car, talking to two boys who sat on the hood. Slowly I cracked my window and pressed my ear against the screen.

"She's not worth all this, Swift," said one boy. "You're a mess."

"No, I'm not," Chris said.

"You made a fool of yourself, man," said the other boy. "She's got a boyfriend. Just forget about her."

Chris waved them away and headed up the walk. He stumbled and my hand flew to my mouth, knocking over the lamp on my desk.

Chris's head whipped up and I stepped back from the window. Shoot. Had he seen me in the dark? I didn't dare look out again, so I hurried to my bed and got under the covers, rolling over so my back was to my door. A few seconds later I heard the front door open and close, then heavy footsteps on the stairs. They clumped down the hall, then stopped. I held my breath and squeezed my eyes closed. The door squeaked opened.

"Erin." His harsh whisper sent a shiver down my back. "Erin. I know you're awake. I saw you." Shuffling feet crossed the carpet. "Just stay out of my damn business." His finger jabbed my shoulder, then his breath warmed my ear. "Got it?" The smell of beer wafted in front of me, and I tried hard not to wrinkle my nose. His mouth stayed close to my ear for, like, fifty years, then he finally straightened up. Giving me a shove, he clumped back across the room and closed the door tightly behind him.

My breath escaped. "Got it," I whispered.

Friday, November 1

Things That Are Not Good 

- I think Chris was drunk last night...must still be bummed out about Amanda...guess I'm lucky...at least I haven't seen Mark kissing anyone and I don't think he has a girlfriend.

- Mark was staring at Jilly at the Halloween party.

- I don't think Mark realizes Jilly doesn't look like that normally. She does not have boobs yet; well just the beginnings of some. Ok, they have gone from nipples poking out (that's about where mine are) to little tiny mounds. But I mean little...check out a Mounds bar and you'll get the idea.

- She also doesn't wear all that makeup. Her mom lets her wear a little eyeshadow and mascara and some blush but that's it. I can't wear any until I'm in 8th grade, which is fine with me. 1 time I tried some and got an ugly rash on my face...SO glad it was in the summer so I could hide out until it was gone. And those were fake eyelashes...she doesn't have platinum blond hair...duh...that was a wig.

Luckily I'm good at hiding my real feelings from Mark....if he knew he'd run howling from the room. If Jilly had seen him without his beast costume, when he wasn't howling at the moon, she might not think he was so immature. They might fall madly in love and I'd never have a chance. I'm, like, dying about Mark staring at Jilly. It's killing me.

Things To Think About

- Mark hasn't asked 1 thing about Jilly and I'm SO glad...but kind of surprised. Maybe he heard what Jilly said about 7th grade boys being immature. Maybe it was just 1 look at the Halloween party and he's forgotten all about her. Whatever the reason, I'm all for it.

- Rosie thinks Tyler Galleon likes me...crazy. No 1 ever likes me. I always like someone and then they like Jilly...the story of my life. Besides, Tyler's a little dorky. Even if he did like me, I don't think I could ever like him back...but he's pretty nice...didn't like him at 1st cuz of his Big Foot comment but he's ok...think he'd look good in a regular old T-shirt and jeans...not those pants that are so big they look like 2 people could fit inside them....And stop with the spikes already...probably has really great hair but u'd never know it under all that gel.

Things That Make Me Happy Right Now

- Omigosh! I just realized something. Mark won't recognize Jilly any more than she would recognize him. I'm saved!

- I can stop stressing about this. Quick! Where's my pillow?

chapter 14

Erin Swift, aka Idiot

Just when I thought it was safe to go to the bathroom again, Serena showed up. I was standing at the sink, checking out a small pimple on the left side of my nose. I was asking myself the Big Question — To pop or not to pop — when Serena walked in. She stopped and glared at me, crossing her arms over her chest.

"How long are you going to be?"

"This is a public bathroom, Serena."

"I want some privacy."

I raised my eyebrow at her, pimple forgotten. "What for?" Was she afraid to let me hear her pee? Or do the other thing?

"None of your business, Swiftless." She glared even harder and tapped her foot. Please. She didn't own this bathroom. I could stay in here as long as I wanted to. I returned to the mirror, running my fingers through my hair, wishing I had the comb that Jilly had given me.

"It won't help," Serena said.

I'd learned my lesson in Round One. I ignored her.

"He likes Jilly. Accept it."

My heart did a funny little twist inside my chest, but I forced myself to continue looking in the mirror, to act as if I hadn't heard or if I had, that I had no idea what she was talking about.

"I saw him staring at her when she went to practice the other day." She was close to me now, our arms practically touching. "She didn't see him but when she does — *wham!*" She slapped the sink for emphasis and I jumped. "It's all over."

She was lying. He didn't know who Jilly was. He couldn't under all the makeup and that wig. My legs quivered. I didn't want my lips to do the same. "Here's your privacy," I said, making for the door.

. . .

"Swift! Wait up!"

I turned to see Mark hurrying toward me, Serena's words pricking annoyingly at the back of my mind. I waved and then turned to sort through the books in my locker, trying to find the novel we were reading for English.

"Ready for another basketball blowout?" Mark asked as he came up beside my locker.

"Ready for the soccer field?" I shot back. "Or I should say, ready for me to kick your butt?" He laughed and I relaxed. Serena. What did she know? So what if he'd seen Jilly again? He hadn't asked about her at all, and it had been four days since the Halloween party. S.W. was just trying to freak me out. But she wasn't going to ruin this friendship.

"It's winter, Swift, in case you hadn't noticed," Mark said. "It should be an indoor sport."

"Wimp." Then I smiled. "Indoor soccer."

He laughed. A slight blush crept up his cheeks.

"What's with you?" I asked, shoving him playfully.

"Huh? Nothing. I was just thinking . . ." His words trailed off.

"Don't hurt yourself," I said.

He smirked.

"Spill it," I said. "Just get it out." I felt a little bit flirty, a little bit friendly.

"Okay," he said. "But I feel kind of weird."

"You look kind of weird but that hasn't stopped you from talking before."

"You're just full of good ones today, aren't you, Swift?"

"Always." I pulled out my books and closed my locker. "Hey, did I tell you my new great idea?" I didn't wait for an answer. "On the 'Meet the Faculty' page, I'm going to have two photos of each teacher, one in profile, like prisoner mug shots. Then I'll put a row of numbers under each of them with a list of their 'crimes.' That would be like their classes and stuff." We turned and headed toward homeroom. "Are you even listening to me?"

"Sorry," Mark said. "I'm a little distracted. Great idea. Mrs. Porter can be the warden."

I laughed at the image.

"Hey, that reminds me," Mark said as we sat down in our seats for homeroom.

"What? You forgot how to create frames on a page?"

"No." He seemed nervous again.

I leaned forward. "So?"

"I've been meaning to ask," Mark whispered, avoiding my eyes. "That girl you were with at the Halloween party? You know." He made a gesture in front of his chest to indicate her boobs. "Are you two, like, good friends?"

My heart sank to the rubber tips of my Chucks.

Erin P. Swift, You Fell for It!

Big time.

Monday, November 4

My life has ended. MARK LIKES JILLY. I can't even believe I was able to type those words. Stab me to death, why don't you? God, I can't believe Serena was right, which is another thing that totally stinks. If something happens with Mark and Jilly, Serena will be in my face about it every day. I'm going to have to transfer schools.

But I should have known. The whole conversation, maybe even our whole friendship, was all a big cover-up for what he really wanted—info about Jilly. Well, I decided right away that if he wanted information, he'd have to fight for it. And of course, he did, which was really annoying.

After he asked the Question That Ruined My Life in homeroom, I tried to avoid him. But he kept asking every time he had a chance. I even had to hide out in the bathroom to get rid of him. Gee. I never thought I'd write something like that . . . getting rid of Mark Sacks. Anyway, he stopped me AGAIN in front of the gym and I told him it was against my religion to talk to a boy without a female relative present . . . no idea where that came from . . . maybe a movie or something, but it confused him enough that I could take off B4 he tried again.

My luck ran out in English when of course he asked again and I pretended I didn't know what girl he was talking about. Then he's like, you know, that girl at the party, the 1 with—and he did that stupid gesture in front of his chest again. Well, I was getting pissed so I'm like, some girl at the Halloween party with—and then I imitated the gesture, hoping he'd see how stupid it was. How stupid HE was. How could he like her? After all the time we'd spent together?

Then he gave me this look, so I'm like, ok, fine. We're friends. What else do you want to know? She has 2 older sisters, Becca and Molly, she goes to Maine every summer to visit her relatives, she likes drama and hates homework. I gave him my biggest, meanest glare and asked him if I missed anything. Know what he said? "Her shoe size." Excuse me? It wasn't enough that he liked my best friend, who he has only seen and never talked to, but he has to start ragging on my feet? He could tell I was mad and said it was just a joke and what was I so bent about. I considered giving him a nose to match Serena's, so it was a good thing the teacher interrupted.

I'm so mad and sad and frustrated, I could scream.

Will I ever know a kiss that doesn't taste like a pillowcase?

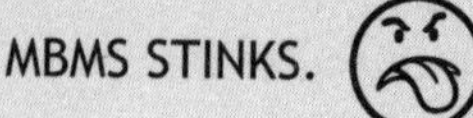

chapter 15

DEFCON 1

"What are you doing in there?" Chris stood with his arms across his chest. I was huddled in my sleeping bag in the basement guest room closet. It seemed smaller than I remembered, with my back shoved up against the back wall and my feet practically sticking out the door, even though I had my knees tucked against me inside the sleeping bag.

"None of your business," I said, my voice cracking. Shifting in my sleeping bag, I reached to close the door.

"Okay." Chris's voice was softer. I looked at him suspiciously. He wasn't looking at me. He was looking at the closet. "This was the DEFCON 4 spot, right?" He leaned forward and looked inside the closet.

"Yeah. Good memory."

He glanced down at me.

"You look like you had more than a DEFCON 4 happen to you." Turning, he crossed the room and plopped down on the bed.

"It's a DEFCON 1," I whispered, feeling my throat close up.

Chris sat up. "DEFCON 1? Wasn't that the O'Learys' tree house?"

I shrugged and looked down at my sleeping bag, picking at a stray thread near the zipper.

"Yeah," Chris said, nodding. "It was. That was a great place to hide out." He looked at me. "But I hated going to get you. It was always at dinner when I was hanging with the guys."

"Sorry," I mumbled.

"No worries," Chris said. "That was a long time ago. Now I just have to drive you everywhere." I glared at him, but he raised his hands to protest. "I was just kidding."

We sat quietly for a few moments, me picking at the thread in the sleeping bag, Chris staring at the ceiling, his hands behind his head.

"How're things?" I had managed to work the thread free, pulling it away from the nylon sleeping bag to leave a winding trail of pinprick holes. I wound the thread around my finger.

"Okay. You know."

"Yeah," I said, realizing that I did.

"Erin?"

I tilted my head to one side. "Hmm?"

"Your finger is purple."

It was true. I'd wound the thread so tight I'd cut off my circulation. Unwinding it quickly, I watched as my finger changed from purple to pink, tingling as it did so. I wiggled it to make sure it still worked.

Chris stood up. "So dinner's gonna be ready in twenty minutes."

I nodded.

"I'm not coming back down to get you."

"I know."

"Good." His voice sounded stern, but his face was soft. Something shiny caught my eye as he walked across the room, something hanging from his belt loop.

The silver basketball key chain.

• • •

I stood outside Ms. Moreno's computer lab by myself. I'd managed to avoid talking to Mark since he had cornered me, pretending I didn't see him trying to catch my eye. But today I would have to sit near him at I-Club because the leaders were having a meeting and Ms. Moreno said we couldn't miss it unless we had a note from the undertaker, which I thought was pretty morbid. I stared down the hallway, hoping Rosie would show up without him, even though they usually came together.

I felt as if I'd won the lottery when I saw Rosie coming up the hallway alone, until I saw the look on her face.

"What's with you and Mark?" were the first words out of her mouth.

"What do you mean?" So he was the type who talked.

"He said you're acting all mad for no reason."

"It's not for no reason," I said, immediately wishing I hadn't. I'd just admitted I was mad and I didn't want her to know that.

"So what is it?"

"Nothing." I couldn't tell her. She and Mark were practically sister and brother.

"Look, I'm not going to say anything if you don't want me to. I just hate to see you two fighting."

I laughed. Me and Mark fighting? It sounded like we were a couple or something.

"He's kind of bummed out about it," Rosie said in a low voice. A few kids passed behind her and went into the lab.

I'm sure he is, I thought. *He doesn't have a direct pipeline to Jilly information now.*

"Hey, Erin."

"Hey, Tyler."

His face lit up like the DSL light on a modem. "Cool shirt," he mumbled as he passed me to go into the lab.

Rosie raised her eyebrows and smiled slyly. "I told you he likes you."

"Shut up," I said, my cheeks warming.

Rosie's attention shifted down the hall. "Here he comes," she said, and I knew she meant Mark. She turned to me. "Look, whatever it is, just work it out, okay? You're both my friends and I'd like it to stay that way." She pulled her backpack off her shoulder. "I'll see you inside."

I stared after her, warmed by the words she'd spoken, freaked by the fact that I was now out in the hallway by myself with Sack o' Potatoes approaching. I tucked my shirt into the back of my pants so I had an excuse to look over my shoulder. Mark was still far down the hall. He raised his arm like he was waving, but maybe he was just stretching.

Mark Sacks, now known as the Boy Who Likes Jilly, Not Me.

I frowned. No way was I going to wave or stretch back. I bent down to tie my shoe that was already tied (one of Jilly's tricks actually coming in handy), watching Mark out of the corner of my eye. I could almost see Jilly hanging on his arm, whispering something in his ear, making him laugh. Or giving him a quick peck on the cheek, the kind that tells everyone, "He's mine, so eat your heart out." But I was the one who made him laugh. I was the one who should be kissing him. Me, me, ME. I wanted to crawl out of my skin or scream at the top of my lungs or both.

He was getting closer.

Rosie had said to work it out. Okay. Let's see. What's the best way to work this out?

• • •

I was getting claustrophobic in the custodian's closet. It was only about five feet by five feet and most of it was covered with supplies. Shelves lined the three walls and they were jammed with cleaners, bleach, and sickly sweet air fresheners. I was shoved up against a vacuum and two brooms, trying not to look at the disposable vomit cleanup kits stacked in front of me. I had considered hiding out in the bathroom but I knew Rosie would probably look for me there, once Mark walked into the lab and I didn't follow. After all, that's where I was when I'd overheard Serena's friends talking about me. I couldn't be predictable if I wanted to avoid more humiliation.

I wondered what they were doing in I-Club. Did they already forget I wasn't there? (Meaning, did Mark even notice I was gone?) Was Tyler making a mess of the faculty interviews he was in charge of? I couldn't believe I was sitting on the floor of a custodian's closet when I could be at a computer, creating web pages. And it was all Mark's fault. And Jilly's. If he hadn't come in the theater, he never would have seen her. And if she wasn't so pretty he never would have noticed her onstage or at the party.

"So what?" I said aloud, when a voice inside pointed out that if I'd had the guts to say no to play tryouts, he would have called me at home with his question, or maybe I would have stayed after that day, too, and we would have worked out the problem together. And then maybe none of this would have happened.

But then again, maybe it would have. He'd seen her at the party. So, it was the party's fault. If we hadn't gone . . . but he had seen her other places, like getting off the bus.

So, it was the bus's fault. If we didn't come to school on the bus, then —

"Stop," I hissed aloud. I was driving myself crazy with all this "if this, then that" stuff. Sighing, I squinted in the dim light of the overhead bulb and adjusted my butt on the floor, elbowing a mop that would have clattered against the wall if I hadn't caught it in time. Jilly was right. A janitor's closet was no place for kissing. Or hiding. The fumes from the cleaning supplies were giving me a headache. I tried holding my breath for a while, then tried making my breaths short and shallow. I felt like I might faint.

I stood up slowly and looked at my watch. Three-forty. I'd only been in the closet a half an hour. I still had another hour and fifty minutes before Mom would come to pick me up. I couldn't stay in here for an hour and fifty more minutes. I'd have to find another spot.

As I reached for the door handle, I heard footsteps down the hall. Quickly I pulled the string, plunging the closet into darkness, the only light coming from the narrow crack between the door frame and the door because I'd left it slightly ajar. I kept my face close to the crack, holding my breath as the footsteps got closer and closer. After a while I couldn't tell which was louder, my pounding heart, or the *clump-slap* of the shoes coming down the hallway.

The clump-slap stopped. In front of the custodian's closet. I stepped back, bumping a broom, which clanged against the metal shelves, knocking down a row of Windex bottles like dominoes. Throwing my arms over my head to protect myself, I sank to the floor, just as the door flew open and the light clicked on.

chapter 16

IPF (Invalid Page Fault)

"Not again," a man's voice groaned.

I pushed away two rolls of paper towels, shoved the Windex aside, and pulled the mop away from my face. Mr. Foslowski stared down at me, hands on hips, scowl on face. Then his expression softened.

"Aren't you the corn girl?"

"Yes," I said, pushing a mop away from my head.

Mr. Foslowski frowned. "Didn't expect this from you." He stepped forward. "Okay, where is he?" He began pulling the supplies off the floor and restacking them on the shelves. He moved a trash can aside and peered under another set of shelves. "Where've you got him hidden?"

"Who?" I asked, standing up to brush myself off. I picked up the rest of the things that had fallen on the ground.

Mr. Foslowski turned to me, eyes narrowed. "Who else?" he said. "The boy."

I smiled nervously. "There isn't one."

"Got to be one somewhere," Mr. Foslowski muttered, pushing aside some rolls of toilet paper. "Why else would you be in here?" I wanted to point out that even the smallest boy couldn't hide behind a roll of toilet paper, but I decided I'd better not. He rummaged around, straightening things as he searched. Finally, he turned around and faced me. "There's no boy in here."

I realized that the only thing more embarrassing than being caught in the custodian's closet with a boy is getting caught in there by yourself. I glanced around, wondering if there was a hidden camera nearby to catch my humiliation on tape.

"No, sir."

"Just you."

"Yes, sir."

"No boy."

"No, sir." I sighed. "No boy at all." And when I said those words, something happened inside me. As if everything I'd ever felt about my non-boyfriend life overflowed. My mouth opened, and a whole gigabyte of words poured out. "Though I wish there was. Well, actually not in here, but maybe somewhere a little more, well, comfortable. Not that this isn't comfortable for all the cleaning supplies, you know, but, well, it's not really designed for people to hang out in, which, of course, is why you kicked out those eighth graders who were in a closet doing — well, you know.

"But there's this boy in my homeroom and English and word processing, who's also in this Intranet Club after school, and we're really good friends even though I like him more than friends, but yesterday he started asking about my best friend and he thinks she's cute and she always gets all the boys, even when she doesn't want them, and it's just not fair." I took a breath, then let it out long and slow. I should have been completely embarrassed saying all of that to a complete stranger, but for some reason I felt . . . relieved. Lighter. Like I'd just defragmented my hard drive. Finally, someone knew about my feelings besides my private web page. It didn't matter that it was Mr. Foslowski. It was out there.

I snuck a peek at him. He was staring at me, chewing the inside of his cheek. He was either going to burst out laughing or smack me for talking too much. But which one?

He didn't do either. Instead, he opened the door wide, pulled out a short step ladder, and sat down. "You say he asked about your best friend?"

Startled, I nodded.

"And he thinks she's cute?"

I nodded again.

"Is she on the same track as the two of you?"

I shook my head no.

Mr. Foslowski raised his fingers to his chin and scratched his goatee. "But you were friends with this boy. Before he said anything about your best friend."

I nodded. Then I told him everything — about how "this boy" was one of the few people who never teased me about the PI, except when he knew I was ready to handle it. How we talked a lot about computers and other stuff, too, and he asked my advice. How he helped me figure out some things, too. The whole time I was talking, Mr. Foslowski just nodded every so often. When I finally stopped, he nodded one last time. "I'd say you're lucky to have this friend."

"But he's not really my friend," I said. "He was just nice to me so he could get to Jilly." I clamped a hand over my mouth. I hadn't used any names until now.

"But you just said you were friends before he knew about Jilly," Mr. Foslowski pointed out. "Right?"

I thought about it. Walked through everything in my mind in the order it happened. "I guess. Maybe."

Mr. Foslowski stood up, folded the ladder, and put it away. "I know you probably won't believe this, but a good friend can be better than a boyfriend." He reached into a jar and held out a cherry Tootsie Pop. "Friends are like a good Tootsie Pop. They last longer." He chuckled. "That is, if you don't bite them."

Or they don't bite you, I thought. Then I sighed. I'd much rather have Mark like me more than a friend. Still, it was true that Mark and

I were friends before he spotted Jilly on the stage that day. But could I be friends with him, knowing he liked Jilly more than a friend? And how fair was that? He didn't even know her. It was all about her looks.

Sighing, I stood up and stepped toward the door. My watch read 4:30. I still had another hour to kill before Mom would be here to pick me up.

"They're still in there working on those computers," said Mr. Foslowski. "I was just over that way."

Until he said that, I had fully intended to find another place to hide until my mom came. But now, suddenly, I had a different plan.

Mr. Foslowski raised an eyebrow. "Want me to walk you over?"

I shook my head. "I know the way." I tucked the Tootsie Pop in my back pocket and strode down the hall. Then I stopped and turned. "Thanks."

A hand appeared out of the closet and waved me away. Taking a deep breath, I put one Chuck in front of the other and kept going.

• • •

"Where did you go?" Tyler was in my face the minute I stepped into the computer lab. He acted like I'd been gone for days, not just ninety minutes.

"I had an emergency thing I had to deal with," I said.

"Is everything okay?" Ms. Moreno had overheard me and her face filled with concern.

"Everything's fine," I said, guilt over the lie poking at me. "False alarm." I attempted a smile. "I don't have a note from the undertaker."

Ms. Moreno returned my smile. "That's okay. I'll catch you up tomorrow."

I nodded and dropped my backpack on the floor next to my computer and got to work. Not once did I glance over at the Mark cluster, though I thought I would leap out of my skin if I didn't at least get one little peek. Once I got into the work, though, I mostly forgot about him. My group asked me questions and I answered them. I whipped the pages into shape, helped Tyler reformat his faculty interviews, and gave some eighth graders a lesson in image mapping. This is where I belonged. This is what I was good at.

"Okay, people, let's wrap it up." Mr. Arnett's voice startled me. I looked up from my computer. It couldn't be time to go. No way. But I could tell by the clock that it was. Of course, I'd only gotten an hour today, instead of the usual two and a half.

"Um, Erin?" Tyler was leaning toward me, still in his seat.

"Yeah, Tyler?"

"I was wondering. Do you want to, could you —"

Oh, no. Was he going to ask me out?

"— show me how to align an image again?"

I looked at him. "Oh. Sure." Funny, I felt a little disappointed, rather than relieved, that he hadn't asked me out or something. What was that about?

By the time I had shown Tyler all three alignment commands, the room was almost empty. The only ones left were Ms. Moreno, Mr. Arnett, Rosie, and Mark. Great.

"See you Thursday," Tyler said as he headed out the door. "She had an emergency," he said to Mark, like he had this inside information he was sharing. I couldn't help smiling as I made sure all the computers in my cluster were logged off.

"So, what was the emergency?" Mark stood between two computers in two different clusters, blocking my exit. He had one thumb hitched under the strap of his backpack and his bangs were flung back, revealing both eyes.

"None of your business," I said, avoiding those eyes.

"Yeah, I guess it isn't." He shifted his feet. "I waved, but I guess you didn't see me."

"I had to go," I said.

"Yeah," he said. "The emergency." There was an awkward pause.

"Look," we both said at the same time. Then we laughed. That helped.

"I'm sorry I freaked out yesterday," I said. "I've just got a lot on my mind."

Mark nodded. "Friends?" He held out the hand that wasn't holding his backpack.

"Friends," I said, grasping his hand. It was warm, firm. The only other boy's hands I'd touched were gross, sweaty ones when Jilly and I went to Skate City and a boy asked us to skate. I never wanted to skate with the boys, but Jilly did. They always seemed to come around in pairs, probably having done some rock-paper-scissors thing to decide who got to skate with Jilly. The loser skated with me.

"Um, Erin?"

"Huh?" I said, my focus back on Mark in the computer lab.

He nodded down at my hand, still clutching his.

"Oh, sorry." My cheeks flamed and I turned away quickly, smacking my backpack into Rosie. "Sorry!" I said.

"That's okay." Rosie looked at both of us. "Did you two kiss and make up?"

It was Mark's turn to blush. I rolled my eyes and shook my head at him, and he smiled. This wasn't so bad. Maybe he figured out why I was mad. Maybe he wouldn't ask about Jilly anymore and he wouldn't see her very much and maybe he'd forget about her.

Maybe computers never freeze and my feet will turn into a size 6 while I'm sleeping.

Tuesday, November 5

FYI, computers DO freeze and my feet did NOT shrink to a size 6 during the night. What does this mean in real life? 1st thing this a.m., Mark asked me Jilly's name. Like I'm going to give out this kind of information. Mark went on to list everything I told him about Jilly, like he hung on my every word when it was about her, but not when it was about my latest web page. Can't he just admire her from afar and not have to know her name, which would make her a real person?

But his cute face was all hopeful, waiting for my answer, so I decided to try doing this friend thing and told him her name, even though I had a large pit in my stomach, about the size of the one you see in movies that several unsuspecting people fall into in the middle of the jungle cuz it's covered with leaves and stuff.

Well, nothing earth-shattering happened when I told him her name...sky didn't fall and he didn't suddenly see me in a new light and forget all about her. Oh, well...wishful thinking. So, I'm trying what Mr. Foslowski said to see if it's true. It's the Great Experiment. The results will no doubt be published widely in the scientific magazines.

PROBLEM:

Which lasts longer, boy friends or boyfriends?
(aka, How long does a Tootsie Pop last?)

This scientist, Erin P. Swift, has 1 thing to say about the Problem—WHO CARES? She wants Mark to declare his love for her.

HYPOTHESIS

Mark will continue to like Jilly, Jilly will fall for Mark, Erin P. Swift will be deleted, tossed in the trash where no 1 will see her, let alone find her and fall madly in love with her.

HYPOTHESIS

If they start going out, it will ruin everything.

Click **Yes** if you agree, **No** if you're an idiot.

chapter 17

Gag Alert

"Cute alert! Attention. Major cute alert."

We were nearly to the school doors when Jilly grabbed my arm, spinning me around. I managed to get a quick peek before stumbling forward. Mark Sacks was about thirty yards away, playing hacky-sack with some boys on the frost-encrusted brown grass. My heart dropped to my ankles. If anyone clicked YES to agree with my hypotheses, they won the prize — a front-row seat to the love match of the century.

"He's okay," I said, adjusting myself. "Come on, let's go inside."

"Okay? Are you kidding? He's a god."

I sighed loudly. "If you like that type." I glanced his way to make sure he hadn't seen us. Then I had an inspiration. "He looks like a seventh grader. You're too mature for him."

"Anyone that cute is worth checking out, no matter what grade he's in," Jilly said. Then she grabbed my arm. "Don't look at him. Just act natural."

"Not this again," I moaned.

"Wait," she said. "I think he's looking at me."

"He's not looking at you. He's kicking the hacky-sack." I was feeling a little antsy. If he looked this way, he would see me. And if he saw me, he might come over. And if he came over, he'd see Jilly. And if he saw Jilly, he'd want me to introduce him. And if I introduced him —

I tugged at her arm. "I'm not going to spy for you, Jilly. Come on."

Jilly stared at me.

"What?" I asked. But I knew what it was. I'd never really talked to her like that before. Stood up to her. "He just kicked it up, caught it in his right hand, and is heading into the building," I said before she could say anything back. "Can we go now?"

Jilly glanced across the lawn. I leaned toward the building, trying to hide us behind a group of boys.

"Hey, Swift!" Dang. He'd seen me. He was halfway across the grass, coming toward us.

"Omigod, he knows you!" Jilly said, then turned a suspicious eye on me. "And you know him. Why were you pretending you didn't?"

"I couldn't really see," I said lamely. "The sun was in my eyes."

"The sun is that way," Jilly said huffily.

"We're going to be late," I said. "Come on."

"I'll catch up," Jilly said, bending down to tie the famous shoe that wasn't untied.

"Whatever," I said. It was over. I'd tried my best but now it was out of my hands. And I wasn't going to hang around and watch them fall into each other's arms and declare their undying love. I'm not into self-torture. As I reached for the door handle, Jilly caught my arm.

"Wait a minute," she said. "You don't like him or anything, do you?"

I avoided her eyes. Like him? That amazing eye peeking out from under that amazing hair? The way his smile was a little lopsided, like we shared a secret? The way he said, "Swiftly," and it didn't make me roll my eyes?

What's to like?

Then a crazy thought crossed my mind. What if I said yes? Came right out with it?

I could see the announcer with the banana-wide grin thrusting a microphone into my face. "Erin Swift, Come Out With It!" he shouts as the studio audience chants, "E-rin, E-rin, E-rin."

I'd squint up through the glaring studio lights at the large box of overripe tomatoes hanging above our heads. If I told the truth and the audience liked my answer, they'd hit their buzzers and the box of tomatoes would splat down on Jilly. But if they didn't like my answer, the box would splat on me.

"Erin?" A lone voice from the audience rose up. "Erin, snap out of it."

I blinked. Jilly was furrowing her brow at me. "You don't like him, do you?"

I glanced up furtively. No box of overripe tomatoes. I could still say it. She might back off, using the you-saw-him-first rule. Or he might see us both and decide I was the one, that his true love had been right in front of him on the basketball court the whole time. . . .

I sighed and rolled my eyes. Yeah, right.

"I didn't think so," Jilly said, then cocked her head at me. "You know, we've been lucky never to have liked the same guy at the same time."

I didn't answer. She didn't know about Timothy Kearns in third grade, Jonathan Jones in fourth, or Bobby Ridge in sixth. She always talked about them first, so I figured she had first dibs. Eventually my feelings faded away, usually before Jilly's did, which helped. And Mark, well, I'd probably stop liking him, too. Someday.

"See you at play practice," I said, leaving Jilly outside with Mark as I pushed through the doors into the stream of kids heading for their lockers. I was so flustered I didn't even notice the person standing next to the doors, staring out the window, until she spoke.

"Told you so."

I turned and gave Serena my evilest, most face-bending glare. "Shut up." I didn't even care if she knew I cared. I just wanted to get away.

Wednesday, November 6

Could my life be any more horrible? Today I'm trying to listen as Mark tells me how great Jilly is after their little rendezvous outside the school this morning, but it isn't easy...Mr. Foslowski is way off on this 1. Being his friend is the WORST. I think Mark thinks I think it's neat that he likes my best friend. He has no idea he is TORTURING me with all his questions and stuff. Somehow it feels like he should know he's torturing me, that he should wonder how I feel, knowing he likes my best friend more than a friend but not me, when I've been totally in love with him since the very 1st day of school. Where is the justice?

Today he asked me if I thought she'd go out with him...like I'm going to do all the work for him. I don't think so. He's like fine, be that way, and I'm like you're a big boy, you can do it...guess that was the wrong thing to say cuz he got all bent and gave me a dirty look...wouldn't talk to me for like the rest of the day. Hello? He's mad cuz I won't be the go-between? I KNEW this would happen. They haven't even officially gone out and already Hypothesis #2 was coming true—this will ruin everything.

So I spent the rest of the class staring at Mark's back...which really stinks because he usually turns around at least 1 or 2 times to make faces at me...not today...oh, he's got this 1 cute curl that just touches the collar of his shirt. It was like that curl was hypnotizing me or something cuz I couldn't stop staring at it...kept wanting to touch it...almost did...but didn't. He mighta thought I was some weirdo on top of being mad at me.

Did I say MBMS stinks? Well, even if I did, I'll say it again.

MBMS stinks. 

chapter 18

FE (Fatal Error)

Apparently Mark got over his stage fright and asked Jilly out without my help because they are now, officially, a couple. In seventh grade this means he walks her to most of her classes, is late to his own, and they call each other every day. It also means my conversations with him will now be 90 percent about Jilly, 10 percent about stuff that really matters. I guess I should be happy he's not mad anymore and is talking to me. But the conversations have not been too exciting. For example, they've been going out for a whopping two days, and this is what I got in homeroom:

Mark: Jillian is really great.

Me: (trying to review for a math test) Um hm.

Mark: Did you know she's going to a drama camp over winter break?

Me: Um hm.

Mark: Oh, I guess you would, since you're friends and all.

Me. Um hm.

Mark: So, where do you think I should take her this weekend?

Me: Over a cliff.

Okay, I didn't really say that, I just thought it. But I was annoyed. I decided to try to steer the conversation in another direction.

Me: How is the sports page coming?

BJM (Before Jilly Madness), this question would have launched Mark into a twenty-minute description of what he and his group were doing on the Intranet. AJM (After Jilly Madness), this is what I get:

Mark: Fine. Do you think Jilly would rather go to a movie or out to lunch?

Scientific American hasn't called yet, but Hypotheses #1 AND #2 are popping out all over the place. I'd barely saved them to disc when they came true. This has to be the fastest hypothesis proof in the history of humankind. And it stinks. The only good thing is that I know Jilly's mom would never let her go on a date with a boy by herself because she's only twelve and three quarters. Neither one of us is allowed to date until we're fifteen or sixteen. I kind of wish I'd said this to Mark because maybe it would shut him up, but I didn't. It's weird how I can be mad at him for liking Jilly, but still like him because he's so cute and nice (when he's not Jillified), and feel sorry for him because Jilly won't be able to go out alone with him — all at the same time.

. . .

"I wonder where Mark is," Rosie said when we sat down at our usual table in the cafeteria. But she said it as if she knew exactly where he was and was wondering if I did.

I glanced at the empty place next to Rosie before popping open my water bottle and taking a big swig. I wiped the back of my hand across my mouth and looked right at her.

"You know where he is."

Rosie hesitated, then nodded. "Do you?"

"Probably with Jilly."

Rosie sighed. It was a sad sigh and for a second, I had this wild thought that she liked Mark, too. But I knew she had her eye on her eighth-grade leader in I-Club. Was that to throw me off so I wouldn't think she liked Mark? Was it just a grand scheme to —

"I didn't want to say anything until I was sure you knew," Rosie said, interrupting my thoughts.

"Why?" But I didn't wait for an answer. Because I knew the answer. "You know I like him." Of course she knew. She was so smart about everything.

"I thought you might," she said softly. "But then you're such good friends, I started to doubt it." She smiled. "You're so calm around him. I'm never like that around a boy I like."

I had trouble picturing Rosie as anything but confident.

"That's because we'd get to talking about computers or something and I'd kind of forget that I liked him." I snatched up a bunch of fries as I told her everything, including how he'd asked all those questions and that's why I got mad. "Do you two talk about Jilly?"

Rosie shook her head. "We don't talk about that kind of stuff. We used to, but he wanted me to do all this stuff for him — kind of like what he asked you to do — and I got tired of it."

"Yeah, I know what you mean." I stared at my hamburger, trying not to imagine what Jilly and Mark might be doing and hoping they weren't in one of Mr. Foslowski's closets.

"At least it's Friday," I said. Two whole days where I wouldn't have to run an obstacle course to make sure I didn't see them together.

"Told you."

I looked up. Serena was standing next to me, holding her lunch tray. "Told you, told you, told you," she said. You'd think she'd be happy, rubbing this in my face. But she looked like she was about to cry.

"Yeah," I said, surprising myself with the lack of irritation in my voice. "You told me."

She'd told me once when she was at the window, and then again yesterday at play practice. Jilly had been late, coming in with her hair all messed up. Serena had taken one look at her, rolled her eyes, and said, "She's disgusting. He's disgusting. Can't they find a janitor's closet somewhere?"

I didn't want to think about them doing what I only did with my pillow.

"I know," I said, before I could stop myself. Omigosh. I had actually agreed with S.W. out loud. What did that mean?

"You don't know anything," Serena said, rebraiding her pilgrim braid over her shoulder. I watched Mr. Trubey rifling through his music. We were going to start any minute.

"I know you're jealous," I said. "You wish it was you in the closet with Mark."

"And what about you?" Serena sneered. "You've been drooling over him since the first day of school! He's, like, the only one in the entire school who can't see it."

I remember freaking out when she said that, wondering if it was true. Wondering if —

"Just ignore her," Rosie said, bringing me out of Freak Out Mode and back to the cafeteria. I watched Serena weave her way to another table. It was weird, but I almost felt sorry for her. At least Mark and I were friends. He still wouldn't even talk to Serena.

. . .

Rosie and I got to the bus at the same time that afternoon and climbed on. She automatically took the seat in front of mine, knowing I was saving it for Jilly. I thought that was pretty cool. We were real friends now and it didn't bother her that I sat with Jilly most of the time.

"Save the spot next to you," I said. "I have a feeling she's going to miss the bus again." Before I left her at her locker this morning, Jilly had asked me to save her a seat.

"I always do," I said, not pointing out that yesterday that spot was empty because she'd missed the bus because she'd been doing I-don't-want-to-imagine-what with I-can't-say-his-name. I had a feeling it would happen again today.

Rosie sat backward so she could see me, her head resting on the back of the seat in front of hers. I sat with my back to the window, my feet hanging out in the aisle. I did not want to catch a glimpse of anything that might happen out there.

"Here she comes," Rosie said. "Looks like she'll make it."

I bit my lip. Don't ask, don't ask. But my tongue seemed to have a mind of its own. "Is —"

"Yeah, he's with her," Rosie said, totally knowing what I was going to say. She gave me a tortured look. "Maybe you should read or something until she gets on."

"Why?" I said, wanting to look but not wanting to look. "Are they holding hands?"

Rosie nodded slowly.

"Are they . . ."

"Do you really want to do this to yourself?"

I sighed. "No. I just need to face it. I need to accept it. He's still my friend, right?"

"Right," said Rosie. "But accepting it doesn't mean you have to have a front-row seat to their . . . stuff."

"Right," I said. I crossed my arms over my chest. "Let's talk about something else."

Rosie brightened. She got on her knees and draped her elbows over the back of her seat. "You've got to come over and see my new computer — it's got all the latest stuff on it."

"I don't want to hear about it," I said. "My mom's is totally the latest and greatest, but the computer for me and Chris is, like, two years old. Ancient."

"A dinosaur," Rosie agreed.

"Hey, guys." Jilly stood in the aisle, nudging my feet. I swung them to the floor and she plopped down beside me. I remembered in one of the romance novels I'd read how the woman glowed when she was in love — gag, gag, double gag. What a bunch of poopola. At least that's what I thought, until I saw Jilly's face. It glowed. And it wasn't that greenish-white glow-in-the-dark color we use at Halloween. This was a soft pink, eyes alight kind of glow. It made my heart sink to my stomach.

"Everyone find a seat," said the bus driver, his hand gripping the handle that closed the door.

"Wait!"

We all looked up. Mark bounded up the stairs, stopping briefly as he scanned every face before spotting the glowing one sitting next to me. He strode down the aisle, leaned over, and kissed Jilly full on the mouth. I was so shocked, I just stared at them, their lips pressed together, their heads turned so their noses nearly touched.

One Mississippi, two Mississippi, three Mississippi.

I had to turn and look out the window for four Mississippi. I didn't know if they would have gone on to five or not because the bus driver started yelling over the "woooooooo" of the crowd cheering them on.

"None of that on my rig! You on this bus, kid? No? Then hop off before I take off."

"You should just come home with me," I heard Jilly whisper.

Mark chuckled. Then I heard another sound that was probably a quick peck and Mark's footsteps moving rapidly down the aisle, clunking down the stairs.

Jilly sighed beside me, but I couldn't look at her. I couldn't look at anything because for some stupid reason, my vision was blurry.

 **Saturday, November 9**

Ok...so remember when I said I was lucky when Chris saw Amanda kiss that guy? Well, FORGET IT. CHRIS was the lucky 1. He was a good 50 feet from where Amanda and that guy were mashing. I was like 5 INCHES from Jilly when Mark planted 1 on her. I thought I would die right there on the bus.

I'm living a nightmare...keep seeing their lips pressed together in my mind, like a song that I've put on continuous loop...playing over and over and there's no Stop button in my brain and I'm about to scream. What happened to Mr. Shy and Blushing??? What happened to the guy who kept asking if I thought she'd go out with him??? Where did this Mr. Cool, I'll-Kiss-You-in-Front-of-the-World guy come from???

I tried to avoid Jilly today...didn't think I could look at GFKG (Glow Face Kissing Girl) without bursting into tears or some other stupid thing. But she said she had a homework emergency and could I please come over right away. Even though it was hard, it was harder thinking that if I kept this up, we wouldn't—couldn't—be friends. I had to figure out a way to deal with this. Homework...Ok, I could talk about homework.

I should have known better.

I only helped her with 2 math problems before she started talking about Mark. She goes, have you seen his ears? Like, duh, I sit behind him in 3 classes. She starts saying stuff about them being "attached" and wasn't that the cutest thing? I couldn't help it, I go, attached? Like, to his head? She ignores me and goes off on his earlobes, how some people have attached earlobes and some are detached and that her sister Molly told her all about it. I guess Molly learned it in her genetics class and was sharing this incredibly exciting information with Jilly, who acted like they were having a discussion about hairstyles or clothes, not EARLOBES. How could she be talking about EARLOBES? That is so stupid. And what does this mean, anyway? They were talking about genes. Were they getting married or something?

That thought just about sent me over the edge, so I took off. I couldn't bear to hear about another of Mark's body parts and what Jilly may or may not think about it.

Strange and Mysterious Things 

Tyler left a not-so-anonymous note in the slot in my locker. I knew it was from him cuz there was a smear of hair gel that smelled just like his head. Carla was dying to know what it said—she found it and knew exactly who it was from, too—but I didn't show her... too personal. But I will share it here cuz I want to remember it in case I lose the original:

If you ever slowed down
long enough to see
what is right in front of you,
you might be amazed
to find out who thinks you are
beyond beautiful.
—An Admirer

Beyond beautiful. No 1 has ever called me beautiful, let alone "beyond beautiful." Well, my dad has (beautiful, without the "beyond"), but he doesn't count. Come to think of it, I don't think anyone has ever called me pretty or even cute. It's a pretty good poem for a geeky nerd-type guy. Hmm. That makes me wonder if he copied it from somewhere. I bet he did. He could never come up with something that good, could he?

He's got nice eyes. But that hair? It's got to go.

chapter 19

Mixed Messages

"Mom says we have to get our shoes today." Chris walked toward me, his basketball smacking back and forth in his hands. It was Sunday afternoon and I was supposed to be cleaning my room. But I had too much to say to myself on my personal, private, no one-will-see-but-me web page.

"Okay." With a click the web page disappeared and I was back at the desktop. I logged off and turned around. "You've got a booger."

"Do not," Chris said, but he pulled his wrist across his nose anyway. "What's that?" He pointed to the disc I had ejected from the drive.

"None of your business," I said, running upstairs to hide the disc in my room.

. . .

Chris knew exactly what shoes he wanted and picked them out and paid for them right away. I needed more time. A shoe was very important when you had feet like mine. Not only did it need to give the appearance of a smaller ped, it had to be comfortable and sturdy. It was a very scientific process.

"I'm going to get a Coke at the food court," Chris said after I pulled out my sixth pair of shoes. He handed me a wad of cash. "Meet me there."

After trying on several pairs, I finally made my purchase. Swinging the bag from my wrist, I headed for the food court. I was so busy trying to swing the bag in perfect circles around my wrist that at first I didn't notice the commotion in front of the Orange Julius. But then I heard a girl's voice, loud and angry.

"— got to be the biggest loser in the world to punch another girl in the nose."

I slunk behind a wall jutting out between a store and the food court and peered around it.

Amanda Worthington stood with her arms crossed, her eyes snapping. Chris was a few feet away, Coke in one hand, shoe bag in the other.

Oh, no. It was back. The PI had come back to haunt me and the entire mall. I pressed against the wall, praying no one had seen me. But curiosity made me sneak another peek.

Chris had put his bag and Coke down and was walking toward Amanda. She stepped back, her expression faltering a bit. Then she regained her glare.

"What? Are you going to hit me, too?" she asked. "Does it run in the family?"

For a second I thought he might. He clenched his fist, then released it.

"Your sister has made my sister's life a living hell since they were five," Chris said. He wasn't going to hit her. Even though I kind of wanted him to, I was proud of him because he was so completely in control, keeping Amanda a little off balance. "Jell-O on her seat, stealing her homework, breaking her "Pioneers on the Prairie" diorama — which, I might add, was one of the best dioramas ever made by a seven-year-old — peanut butter in her backpack, cutting off her hair —"

Chris continued his litany, but I had stopped listening. All those times I'd run to one DEFCON or another, he had known why. He knew them all, each and every humiliation. He had been there with me and I hadn't even known it. Maybe that's why he always came to get me. Complaining and whining about it, but he'd always come.

"The whole thing could have been left between the two of them," Chris continued. "But then your sister had to get her little sidekicks to put up those stupid posters all over the school."

I cringed. I hadn't told anyone in my family about the posters. But of course Worthlessness had blabbed it to her sister, who had blabbed it to the whole high school.

Amanda laughed. "She deserved it."

"She never deserved any of it," Chris said quietly. He looked around at her group of friends, some of whom had stepped a little away from Amanda. "There are a lot of things I could say or do right now that *you* might deserve," he said. "But that would make me like you. And that's the last thing I want to be."

There was a low whistle from a couple of boys sitting at a table. A girl at the counter said, "Right on."

Chris picked up his stuff and turned away, spotting me immediately. He strode over and Amanda stared after him, twisting up her face in a way that made her quite ugly. She shouted a few choice names at him and I heard her mutter, "Like it matters what Chris Swift thinks." Funny, but it kind of sounded like it did matter to her. Just a little.

Chris rolled his eyes as he passed me. "Let's get out of here." I hurried after him, my throat tight.

"Chris —"

He waved me away. "Don't say anything."

"But I —"

His gesture stopped my mouth in mid-word.

"Okay, okay," I said. I'd just have to wait until the right time to let him know how I felt.

"I am so over her," he muttered as we got in the car.

"I think her boobs are fake," I said out of the blue.

"Probably," Chris said, putting the car in reverse. "Which may explain her rather poor attitude. Silicone is toxic. They probably got mixed up and put some in her brain, too."

I laughed. "Toxic ooze on the brain."

"A toxic ooze brain stain." We were warming to our subject.

"A toxic ooze brain stain with no pain," I said.

"Don't drain that brain stain or we may all go insane." We laughed hysterically. We kept it up all the way home. I couldn't remember the last time I'd had so much fun with my brother.

When we got home, we swapped high fives. "Thanks for punching Serena," he said. "If you hadn't, I never would have gotten to do that today."

"You're welcome," I said, and we both laughed again.

"Oh, good, you're back," Mom said when we came inside. "Jilly's been calling, Erin. She sounds a little desperate." Mom looked at the clock and so did I. Four. "You can go over for about an hour and a half but then you need to clean your room."

I had talked to Jilly at nine this morning. Of course she was desperate. She hadn't been able to talk to anyone about Mark for seven hours. She needed to moon over him to a live body. But I didn't want to go. I was having fun with Chris.

"Maybe I should do my room now," I said.

Mom looked at me strangely. "I thought you would want to go to Jilly's."

"Oh, I do, but I just feel bad that I didn't do my room when I was supposed to."

Mom walked over and put her hand on my forehead. "You don't have a fever."

I pushed her hand away. "Mom."

She laughed. "Well, you have to admit it isn't like you to give up time with your best friend to clean up your room."

I sighed. There was really no way out of it. "I'll be back in an hour."

• • •

"Tell me again what he was wearing Friday."

I tried not to groan as I leaned against her closet door, hands shoved in my pockets. Jilly asked this every day, even though she saw him every morning when we all got off our buses.

"I don't really notice what he's wearing," she would say. "I'm just looking into his eyes."

Gag, gag, double gag.

"Well? Was he wearing his khaki pants?" Jilly sat on her bed, legs crossed, looking at me as if I was about to deliver news of her Academy Award nomination. I hated the way she said "his khaki pants," like she knew his whole wardrobe and was mentally selecting clothes out of his closet or drawers.

I shook my head. "No. Jeans, Gateway T-shirt, and Asics." I threw my leg over the chair at her desk, straddling it as I rested my arms over the back.

Jilly sighed and I knew she was imagining Mark in this stunning outfit.

"What did he have for lunch?"

"Don't you talk about these things when you meet between classes and after school?" For people on different tracks at opposite ends of the school, they managed to see a lot of each other.

"No. We have more important things to do." She grinned wickedly and I looked away. It had taken days for me to get the image of my best friend and the love of my life with their lips locked together out of my mind. I didn't want a rerun.

"Pizza and a Coke from one of the kiosks," I said in answer to her lunch question. Afterward he had eaten two Starburst candies — cherry and strawberry, from the original flavors. I didn't tell her this part. Those are my two favorite Starburst flavors and I just wanted to keep this important connection between Mark and me to myself.

"So you ate lunch with him?"

"I was at the same table. With Rosie."

"You're getting to be good friends with her, aren't you?" Jilly asked. I would have welcomed a subject change but not this one. Even though it didn't make any sense, I felt guilty for having Rosie for a friend.

"Mark's really good friends with Rosie," I told her, deciding I'd rather be in the agony of talking about Mark than the discomfort of having another friend besides Jilly. "They've known each other forever."

Jilly's face lit up. "Really?"

Uh-oh. I could see the wheels turning inside Jilly's head. Rosie was best friends with Mark. Rosie would know about Mark. Jilly would use Rosie to find out about Mark.

Rosie was going to kill me.

 **Saturday, November 16**

Well, I was right. Yesterday on the bus, Jilly followed Rosie to her seat like a puppy. When she came back she was all, Rosie's kind of snotty, isn't she? And I'm like, no, maybe she doesn't like to play go-between. Then Jilly goes, I like to play go-between, like that meant everyone should like it. Then she launched into how cute Mark was and didn't I just love the way his bang fell over 1 eye like that (I noticed it 1st, on the 1st day of school. That eye and those bangs were MINE), and did I see his butt in those pants? (No, you can't see any butt in those baggy jeans. But I'd seen him in gym shorts, so THERE, Jillian Gail Hennessey).

Is it a crime to strangle your best friend when she won't stop talking about a boy? I think there must be some exception when it comes to situations like this. She just wouldn't stop. Ok, maybe I don't want to strangle her but a nice muzzle would help...or a filter that would only let in conversation that had nothing to do with Mark...easy to set up...anything with Mark text in the subject or body of the conversation would be sent to the Trash. Then Jilly and I could have a normal friendship again...a quiet 1, though, if she couldn't talk about Mark.

The worst part is that I never see her anymore, except after play practice when we go home together. And when I do see her she's babbling on and on about Mark...it's like I don't even know her. She's liked boys B4 but not like this...keeping track of how many times they've kissed and where and how long it lasted and whether they used tongues and I had to tell her to stop cuz I really didn't want to know anymore. Geez. I'd seen enough on the bus.

I cried all over my pillow last night, so I couldn't even practice kissing, even if I'd wanted to. Which I didn't. Not when Jilly was getting to actually kiss the real thing. It was 2 pathetic.

chapter 20

No Strings Attached

I never thought I'd say I was glad for *A Harvest to Remember,* but this week I was because Jilly was more obsessed with her part than she was with Mark. Since we had dress rehearsal and the performance next Tuesday night, she was rehearsing day and night, with and without me.

I, on the other hand, was trying to figure out how I could go to both the dress rehearsal and the computer lab, because my team was counting on me to help them get everything ready.

Wednesday afternoon I stood in the back row of the Vegetable Medley, waiting for our cue to sing the opening song. Once I sang that, I could sneak away before having to be back for my line in about forty minutes. This would be a test to see if I could make it back during the dress rehearsal next week.

I turned slightly so I could see Mr. Trubey through my eyeholes. Our costumes were amazing — they were made out of foam rubber and looked real. But the ear of corn costume was like being inside a toilet paper tube. I could only take small baby steps, though I did have my arms free, which helped.

When our song was over, I shuffled off the stage and down the hall. I had no peripheral vision so I kept knocking into lockers when I got too close to one side. I finally figured out that if I kept to the middle of the hall, I would be okay. I felt like Scout in *To Kill a Mockingbird* (probably the only black and white movie I liked), trying to get home after her school play where she was a ham. I hoped no one was lurking, waiting to jump me.

"Hey, look! Corny's here!" Steve shouted as I shuffled into the lab a few minutes later.

"Erin the Corncob!" said Tyler. "Get your kernels over here and help me."

I smiled inside my costume. I still couldn't believe this semi-nerdy boy had written that beautiful poem about me. I had never said anything to him and of course he never brought it up. But sometimes I thought of the words, which I knew by heart now, and marveled at how a spiky gel head could have written it.

And I would never admit to anyone that I liked Tyler's teasing, his easy way around me now. I wondered if he was more comfortable because he had stopped liking me.

I wondered why the thought made me a little sad.

"Wait, can I have her first?" Mark asked. I glanced over at him. "I need your opinion on this layout," he said, pointing to his screen.

I frowned, wondering if he just wanted to gush about Jilly. I looked over at Tyler, who shrugged and nodded.

"So what's up?" I asked Mark.

"Do you think it looks better with the photos vertical down the left side and the text next to it?"

"Are you kidding?" I said. "You should have had this done a week ago. Hello? We're launching in one week."

"This is one of the last things I have to do," Mark said. "Chill out and check it out." He clicked the mouse a few times and the images loaded. "Or horizontal."

"Wait," I said, grabbing his hand before he could click again. "I need to look at this one first." My eyes jumped from the images to the text, taking in the whole effect. "Okay," I said, lifting my hand from his, "You can click now." I shifted so I could see him out of my eyeholes.

He had a weird expression on his face.

"What are you looking at?" I asked. "Are you going to make a corn joke?"

He smiled. "No. I just —" He seemed flustered and I had no idea why. I realized that I'd briefly held his hand and no electricity had shot up my arm. But I didn't have time to think about it because he had clicked the mouse. "Okay, here's the horizontal."

After I'd made my recommendation — vertical — I headed over to Tyler. I watched as he moved the mouse around. He had nice hands. His nails were short but not too short, and trimmed, which kind of surprised me.

Shrugging off the feeling I had about Mark, I leaned over Tyler's shoulder. "I only have ten minutes," I said through the mouth hole. "Show me what you've got."

• • •

"I think Mark is losing interest." It was the Sunday before the performance, the Sunday before we launched the Intranet, and Jilly and I were in my room, doing our nails. Well, Jilly was doing her nails. I was sprawled across my bed, below my Denver University Pioneers women's basketball team poster, using my mom's laptop to make more changes to the MBMS Intranet pages. Launch was in three days and I still had a lot to do. I was also performing a manicure the Erin way — biting the tips off.

Her comment made me stop in mid-nip.

"What?" I said, not sure how I felt about this. "It's been, like, what? Two weeks?"

"And three days, and about" — she looked at her watch — "ten hours and forty minutes." She turned from my desk, which stood beneath my window because I liked to look out and see what was going on in the real world while I was doing my homework.

"Not that you're counting." I sat up, pushing the laptop aside.

"It's not funny, Erin. I like him. I think." She stood up and walked around the room. "Why don't you have a mirror in this room?"

I shrugged, glancing at the tall dresser in the corner. Even if you put a mirror over it, you would barely be able to see your face. And I refused to have one of those full-length mirrors behind my door because looking at myself all at once like that was just too overwhelming.

"So you still like him?" Two weeks was pretty average for her. It occurred to me that I hadn't really noticed the signs this time. Too busy with I-Club. Maybe she had started to lose interest and I just hadn't made the connection. And Mark had been talking to me more, joking around. And that look when I'd lifted my hand off of his . . .

"Why are you asking that question?" Jilly furrowed her brow at me. "I just said I did."

"You were kind of flirting with Bus Boy on Friday," I said.

"His name is Jon and I was not flirting." Jilly blew on her nails and held them out. "He asked me a question and I answered it." She glared at me. "It was not flirting."

"Okay, okay." I held my hands up like in surrender.

Jilly sighed and moved back to my desk, dipping the brush into the polish. "So I think Mark's going to break up with me, which means I need to break up with him first."

"Why can't you break up together?"

"You can't do that. Someone always has to go first." She shook her head at me. "You don't know anything about this, Erin."

I frowned. Just because I'd never had a boyfriend didn't mean I couldn't have an opinion on the right way to break up. "Maybe not, but I don't see why you have to make a big production out of it."

"I'm not making a big production out of it. I just need to plan what I'm going to say." She licked her lips and turned back to the desk. "And once we break up, you know you can't be friends with him anymore, right?"

I wasn't sure I had heard her right. I crawled to the edge of the bed and sat up, flipping my legs over the side. "What?"

"Look, you've never been friends with one of my boyfriends before, so this is kind of a weird situation. But how would it look if you were still friends with him after he dumps me or I dump him?"

"It would look fine," I said. "Because we were friends long before you went out."

Jilly swiveled around in the chair. "But it'll look like you're loyal to him and not me."

"That's crazy, Jilly. You're my best friend. Everyone knows that."

"I don't like the idea that you'll still be talking to him after I won't be."

Ah. The truth comes out.

"But you won't like him anymore, so why should it matter?" I thought this was perfectly logical. But apparently my inexperience had led me down the wrong path. In love, everything was illogical.

Jilly sighed, then spoke as if to a child. "Because you might be talking about me, and that would be very weird."

I rolled my eyes. "You may find this hard to believe, Jilly, but not every conversation I have with Mark is about you. In fact, none of the conversations I have with Mark are about you." Okay, I was lying a little, but lately that was true. "Do you know why? Because we have a lot in common that has nothing to do with you, which is why we were friends before you started going out and which is why we'll keep being friends when you stop going out."

Jilly's eyes flashed and she pushed away from my desk. I noticed her left hand had only two fingernails painted. "I can't believe you just said that." She stood up, waving her half-painted fingers at me. "A real friend would never be friends with her best friend's ex-boyfriend, even if they were friends before the ex-boyfriend was even a boyfriend to become an ex."

I stood up, facing her head-on. "A real friend would never ask her best friend to stop being friends with her ex-boyfriend when that friend was friends with the ex-boyfriend before he became a boyfriend and is about to become an ex."

We faced off like two boxers in the ring. Jilly put on her stone face. "It's either him or me, Erin."

"Why should I have to pick?" I protested. "Why can't I be friends with both of you?"

"Because you can't be friends with my ex-boyfriend and still be friends with me. That's just the way it is. It's part of the friends-boyfriends-ex-boyfriends code." She put her hands on her hips. "So, who will it be?"

I stared at her. How could she put me in this position? It was crazy.

My thoughts churned around until they settled into one very perfect, very crystal-clear thought. "I choose not to choose," I said.

Jilly frowned. "You can't."

This crystal-clear thought gave me courage. "Yes, I can, Jilly. It's part of the Erin-is-no-longer-a-puppet code. Because you know what? Serena was right. You've kind of always been in charge, and I was always doing what you asked, hardly ever speaking up, letting you sign us up for things, pick our seats in class, decide what we'd do on the weekends. But not anymore." I took a breath, then hurried on before I lost all my courage. "I choose not to choose between you and Mark. That's my choice. It's your choice whether you want to keep being my friend or not." I crossed my arms over my chest. I hoped I looked tough and defiant, because I had crossed my arms to keep her from seeing how much I was shaking.

Jilly stared at me for a full ten seconds. I know because I counted in my head — one Mississippi, two Mississippi, all the way up to ten Mississippi.

"Fine," she said quietly. I'd never heard her speak that quietly before. It scared me. I watched her pick up the nail polish and slowly twist the cap back on. My throat closed up as she slipped on her coat. My eyes stung and I opened my mouth to take it all back, to tell her I was joking, that I was still me, Erin Penelope Swift, her friend since kindergarten. But then that would mean I was still Erin the Corncob, Erin the Puppet, Erin the Go-Along. Erin who everyone else saw. Not me.

I pressed my lips together and watched her walk out of my room. I stayed in the same place, my arms wrapped around myself in a crazy self-hug, holding myself up as I listened to her footsteps on the stairs. One, two, three, four, five, six . . . muffled good-byes from my parents . . . seven, eight, nine, ten, eleven . . . the front door opened, then closed.

My legs gave out beneath me. Dropping onto my bed, I let the sobs escape at last.

Sunday, November 24

Jilly is not my friend anymore. I can't believe it. She just walked out. Just like that. Out the front door and out of my life...my insides are going to explode...I can't breathe. I'm going to drown in not breathing.

I can't believe she asked me to pick between her and Mark. I can't believe she left when I wouldn't pick. I can't believe it. I can't believe it. I can't believe it.

I can't write anymore.

11:00 p.m.

I can't sleep. I keep playing the scene over and over in my head...Jilly's face, her hands on her hips, waiting for my answer. I'm not sad anymore...I'm mad...furious.

She EXPECTED me to pick her. She expected me to do the thing she wanted me to do. And when I didn't, she stomped out like a little baby who didn't get her way. Well, for all I care, she can stomp all the way to Timbuktu.

She totally thinks she's in charge of our friendship and I have to do whatever she says. I AM NOT A PUPPET. And she's not my master puppeteer. Doesn't she get that? She has got to be the most selfish, stuck-up, my-way-or-the-highway person in the entire world.

I am so mad my fingers are shaking as I type this. I'm glad you and Mark aren't going out anymore, Jilly. When he starts to like me I will flaunt it in your face. I'll kiss him right in front of you and you won't be able to pretend it doesn't bother you, even if you don't really like him anymore. I'll tell Bus Boy how you make me sniff your shoulder to check for BO and how sometimes you're still afraid there are monsters under your bed so you leap from the edge of your rug to your mattress, usually hitting your shin on the sideboard. That's why you wear pants so much...so no 1 will see the bruises from trying to get away from monsters that aren't there. You're such a baby.

Do you hear me, JILLY????????

I will never do anything you say as long as I live. You are not my friend. You never were my friend.

I hate you.

chapter 21

Creamed Corn

Jilly and I avoided each other as if we had mono. We both waited until the last possible minute on Monday to get to the bus stop so we wouldn't have to be near each other. I sat with Rosie, and Jilly sat with Bus Boy (I couldn't think of him as Jon).

"You'll kiss and make up," Rosie said when I told her about the BFB (Best Friend Blowout).

"I'm not going to be the first," I said. My monster sob session the night before had cleaned out all the sad stuff. Now I was just mad. "I was right and she was wrong and there's no way I'm going to apologize."

Rosie nodded. "And she's sitting up there thinking the same thing."

"There's no way she could ever think she was right if she really thought about it." I was already planning a JILL-O-RAMA page for my personal website. I would list all of the times she had made me do things I didn't want to do, and include a "Click here" to see who agreed with me or with her.

"Don't make yourself crazy," Rosie said. "It'll work out." Rosie crossed one leg over her knee. "My mom always says that no one can make a fool out of you without your permission."

I thought about this. "Exactly. Jilly made a decision to be foolish and stop being my friend. I didn't make her."

"No, you didn't. Just like she never made you try out for the play, or walk to her house first, even though your house is closer to the bus stop."

I sighed deeply. "I know." I hated thinking about that. After my big speech to Jilly, the last several years rolled through my mind and I saw all the things I'd done for Jilly that I didn't want to do, all the times I'd been too afraid to say something for fear she'd stop being my friend.

But I also remembered the fun times. Like when we hid under the covers with flashlights and looked at *How to Talk to Your Child About Sex,* laughing at the pictures. Or when she surprised me on my birthday with a new WNBA basketball. Or when she sprained her ankle and I did her fingernails without her asking me, even though normally I can't sit still long enough to do stuff like that.

"People always say to stand up for yourself," I said. "But when I finally did, I lost my best friend."

"She'll come back," Rosie said.

"And if she doesn't?"

Rosie looked at me, then out the window. I didn't want to think about what that meant.

When we got to school, Rosie stood up and gave me a friendly punch in the arm. "Remember, you've got to be a corncob tomorrow night. And you've got an Intranet to launch."

"I know." That was the only thing keeping me from running screaming from the house and back to Jilly's doorstep, where I wanted to scream and shout and yell at her for being so stupid. But there was still a ton to do before we could actually click PUBLISH on Wednesday, so the Scream Fest would have to wait. I was spending every extra hour I could after school in the computer lab.

"I've still got three sections to create," Tyler said to me when I got to the lab that afternoon. His voice cracked with anxiety. "How can I get them done in time?"

"My interviews still aren't ready," I said. "And Rosie's group keeps having their images disappear. It's a nightmare." I looked around the room, where kids were clicking frantically, running to other computers, pulling Mr. Arnett or Ms. Moreno over for a consultation. We all felt the pressure. People had been talking about it for the last two weeks, waiting excitedly for the Intranet to go live. Terminals were being installed at different locations throughout the school so kids could access it without having to go into a classroom or to the lab. It was a BIG deal and we all knew we needed to deliver.

And I could never get to my own stuff because people were always asking me for help.

"We can do it," I said to Tyler, knowing that no matter how long I stayed here, I'd still have to work at home tonight and tomorrow night to get it all finished.

• • •

The night of the grand performance of *A Harvest to Remember,* I was desperate for it to be over so I could copy the last of my files to the MBMS Intranet. I had been up until almost midnight the night before, adding the last of the faculty interviews and editing the web logs. With the disc safely tucked inside my backpack, I was ready to upload it to the server. I had trouble concentrating on the play and I thought I might spontaneously start boiling in my costume, melting into Erin soup before I could escape. But I stayed alert, breathing a sigh of relief after I said "I can't heeaarr you" with my hand cupped to my ear. Now it was smooth sailing. I just had a few more songs to sing with the Vegetable Medley.

When the play was over, my parents hugged and congratulated me. Chris made corn jokes but said he liked it.

"Even Worthington was pretty good."

"Yeah. She was." It was true. She might be a snot, but she was a good actress. Almost as good as Jilly.

"Jilly was great," he added, as if reading my mind. I kept quiet. Only Mom knew about our fight, but she hadn't said anything since I'd had to explain my red and puffy eyes the morning after the BFB.

"Did you see Amanda?" I asked quietly. She had shown up with that same boy she was kissing outside the library.

Chris shrugged. "Old news."

I scanned the gym for Jilly and her parents but couldn't see them with everyone milling around. They were probably backstage taking pictures of the Star. She hadn't made eye contact with me once during the play, which she'd done all through rehearsals. But I couldn't worry about that now. After the cast party I had to upload my files and make some final adjustments. I had an Intranet to launch tomorrow.

As my family continued to talk about the play, I saw a pair of arms waving frantically across the gym. Tyler.

"Everything is basically ready," Tyler said, out of breath as he hustled over. "We need your disc."

I turned to my mom. "My backpack's in my locker. I'll meet you guys back in the drama room for the party."

"I can get it," Tyler said. "Go to the party." I shook my head, which meant shaking the entire cob. I wasn't about to give him my locker combination. I liked the poem, but who knew what other strange declaration of love he might put in there? Besides, I had to change anyway.

"I'll get it," I said. "It won't take long." We left the gymnasium and headed down the hall, Tyler several strides ahead of me. I made him turn his back while I dialed my combination, then pulled out my backpack. I reached in the front pocket and shoved the disc at Tyler. "I'll come by after the party to make sure everything's okay."

"Okay. I'll walk back partway with you." As we shuffled back toward the drama room, I heard someone running behind us. *Wham!* I fell forward, my right arm pinned beneath me. Pain shot through my forearm and I cried out, feeling a little lightheaded.

"Watch where you're going, Corn dog." Serena's voice seemed far away.

"You're the one who bumped into her." Tyler's voice seemed equally far.

I tried to move but I was twisted inside my costume, my arm still pinned, the eyeholes now on the side of my head. "Corn dog?" Serena said. And then, "Erin?"

"My arm," I said. "It really hurts."

I could feel someone kneeling beside me.

"It might be broken," Tyler said.

"Oh, God," Serena said. The next thing I heard was footsteps running, running away until I couldn't hear anything except my hot breath inside my costume.

• • •

"It looks like she has a slight fracture," the doctor said as she stepped into the room, holding an X-ray. My parents stood by the examination table, and Chris sat in a chair flipping through *Sports Illustrated.* My brother was obviously deeply concerned about my injury.

"Great." I looked down at my throbbing arm. "Serena just barreled right into me," I told my parents. "Then she told *me* to watch where I was going."

"If it makes you feel any better," Mom said, "she felt really bad about it. She called us here to check on you."

"It doesn't make me feel better," I said. "She's probably worried I'm going to sue her. She's trying to butter us up."

"Now, Erin."

I glanced at her. "Did anyone else call?"

Mom shook her head. "No, honey. I'm afraid not." She knew I meant Jilly.

I sighed and looked at the doctor. "Do I have to have a cast?"

"Yes, you do, young lady," the doctor said. "It'll be on for a few weeks." She turned to my parents. "You should keep her home tomorrow. It will probably still be painful and she should rest."

"I can't rest," I said. "I have an Intranet to launch."

"It'll have to launch without you," said the doctor. "You need to stay home."

I looked to my parents for help, but they had turned into the Not Understanding Parents again. Funny, but this time I wanted to go to school.

"Sorry, Erin," my dad said. "We know this was important to you."

"No, you don't," I practically shouted, then cringed as a sharp pain shot up my arm. "You have no idea how hard I worked on this. I'm the leader. I know the most of anybody. I designed the whole layout. It's *my* Intranet." I knew I sounded like a baby, but they couldn't possibly understand how much it meant for me to be there. This was something I'd signed up for and done all by myself. Without Jilly. It was all mine. And now this doctor and my parents were going to take it away from me.

"I'm going to school tomorrow," I said through clenched teeth. "It's the last day before the Thanksgiving break. It's launch day."

The doctor exchanged a look with my parents. "Let's get that cast on."

• • •

I woke up the next morning with my arm still throbbing. For a drowsy moment I forgot what had happened and almost whacked myself in the head with my cast when I raised my arm. I shook my head as I caught sight of the alien Chris had drawn on the yellow gauze-like plaster. Its big black eyes stared back at me. "The Intranet was *my* thing," I told the alien. "Most of the ideas were mine and Mark's. I was supposed to be there to click PUBLISH."

The alien didn't say a word. I rolled my eyes at it and sat up in bed.

"You're finally awake." Mom came in carrying a glass of water and a pill. "I turned off all the ringers on the phones so they wouldn't disturb you and I wouldn't be tempted to answer and get distracted."

"You turned off my alarm." I looked at her accusingly as I took the pill and glass from her. I glanced at the clock. 11:00 A.M. They'd clicked PUBLISH at 9:00 A.M. The whole school had probably accessed a computer and seen all my hard work. And I wasn't there.

"Actually it went off and you slept through it. Thank goodness. I should have checked it last night." She brushed my hair off my forehead. "How's your arm?"

"Still hurts," I admitted. "Did you check messages?" I wondered if anyone had called to tell me about the launch. Rosie would have. And Tyler. Maybe even Mark. Not Jilly, of course. She could care less, I'm sure.

Mom shook her head. "I'll bring the phone in and you can check them yourself."

I nodded.

"Oh, I almost forgot." She crossed over to my dresser and pulled a jewel case off the top. "I found this in a stack of books next to the computer this morning." She smiled as she held it out. "I don't think they can publish to your Intranet without this."

I took the case from her. *Erin's stuff,* I had printed neatly across the case. *PRIVATE.*

"I bet they postponed the entire thing, honey. Don't you feel better now?"

"Thanks, Mom, but this is —" I stopped. Something on the disc, which I could see through the smoked plastic cover, caught my eye. I grasped the edges of the case, my fingers trembling. Slowly, I lifted the lid.

MBMS Intranet was written clearly across the silver surface of the disc.

My heart stopped beating. I had put the discs in the wrong cases. I had given Tyler the wrong disc to upload to the server.

My personal, private, no-one-will-see-but-me web page had been published for the entire MBMS population.

chapter 22

OMIK (Open Mouth, Insert Keyboard)

OH. MY. GOD.

I spent the next half hour hyperventilating. I kept closing my eyes and opening them again, each time hoping the disc in my hands would say *Erin's Stuff — PRIVATE.* I must have done this twenty times before the reality sunk in. This meant that Mark Sacks, the Cutest Boy in the Universe, had read in my private blog that I thought he was the cutest boy in the universe. That I wanted to kiss him, or maybe even his feet. And I'd called him a hot tamale. He knew everything about me. He must think I'm the stupidest girl in the world.

And I wrote about PILLOW KISSING.

OH. MY. GOD.

Wait a minute. Someone must have caught the mistake. They wouldn't just publish it without checking my content. Or maybe they had decided to wait for me. My heart slowed down. Of course. I was getting freaked out for nothing. They were waiting for me or if not, the teachers checked. Everything would be all right. Right?

Wrong. Dead wrong. Twenty minutes later my hands stopped shaking long enough for me to check voice mail. There were fifty-seven messages. Fifty-seven. Fifty-seven people calling after my private thoughts were broadcast all over the school. Fifty-seven people I hadn't known were calling because Mom had turned all the ringers off. I guess I was glad I found out about the disc switch before I checked our messages.

"To listen to your messages, press one." The voice startled me. My finger hesitated over the 1, then I closed my eyes and pressed.

"This is Tyler. Or, as you like to call me, Geeky-Nerdy Tyler. I just want you to know that you're really mean and I can't believe I actually thought you were my friend." *Click.*

"To delete this message, press six. To save it, press eight." I pressed 8.

From Serena: "You are the most hateful person in the entire universe. Everyone is asking me if they can come to the S.W. Hate-o-Rama. Guess what? I'm developing an Erin Swift Hate-o-Rama that's going to be on the INTERNET, not just a stupid school Intranet. So the whole world will know what a horrible person you are." *Click.* I pressed 8 again.

"Erin? This is Carla. Gosh, I don't know what to say. I'm sorry. I'm surprised by some of the things you said. But I feel bad for you, too. Um, I guess that's all." *Click.*

From Tyler again: "I can't believe you typed that poem for the entire school to see. You are cruel and heartless. I feel very sorry for the person who wrote it, which by the way was NOT me, but I feel sorry for me, too, because since your stupid website says I wrote it, everyone thinks I did and is making fun of me. Thanks a lot."

From Tyler a third time: "And even if I did write that poem and did NOT copy it but wrote it from scratch with NO help from anyone, don't think any word of it was true. It was opposite day when I wrote it. So what it really says is 'If you ever sped up fast enough to smell what is right behind you, you might be unsurprised to find out that foul stench is you.'" *Click.*

Tyler's last call was brief: "And it's signed, Your Enemy."

Foul stench? How many twelve-year-olds knew those words? It

was one of my favorite phrases. Ever since I'd heard it during the first *Star Wars* which was really the fourth, when Princess Leia says to Governor Tarkin on the Death Star, "I recognized your foul stench when I was brought onboard."

Foul stench. I had loved it until someone used it against me. Tyler's new version of his poem really hurt. It was so mean. Really mean. I knew the stuff I'd said had hurt him, but didn't he realize it wasn't meant for everyone to see? Didn't anyone realize that? And didn't he see that I'd said he had nice eyes? What about that?

And I said that Serena was right about Mark liking Jilly. Didn't she read that part? True, I had an entire page devoted to the S.W. Hate-o-Rama and only one line on another page about her being right, but still. Why does everyone dwell on the negative?

I sank deeper under my covers as I listened. There were messages from people I didn't even know. Some saying I was right about Serena, others saying I was the mean one. And still others keyed in on specific things I'd written.

"Am I a hot tamale?" one caller asked before laughing and hanging up.

"I might kiss you for six Mississippis . . . if you gave me a million dollars!" *Click.*

I was amazed at people's brutal honesty. Didn't they think about the possibility that my parents might pick up the messages first? Obviously not, because they all were letting loose with their own feelings.

"Right on about Serena. What a b----."

"Jilly may be a little bossy but she's nice, too. I can't believe you'd say things about your best friend like that. My best friend, Caroline Crouse, has BO and sometimes really bad breath but you don't see me broadcasting it all over the school." *No, just to my voice mail,* I thought.

"Serena is not mean to everyone, you know." Obviously from a Serena groupie.

One message was particularly surprising.

"Um, Erin? You don't know me but I'm on your track and in one of your classes and um, well, Ikissmypillowtoo." *Click.* She said the last part so fast I had to replay it to make sure I got it right. Someone else out there kissed her pillow. I found that comforting.

Several people called to tell me they had clicked YES, that they agreed with my predictions about Mark and Jilly. One boy even added a third option, "I clicked WHO CARES? because you girls are always crying about which boy doesn't like you and it's really stupid. Why do you care so much? You're pathetic." Obviously a boy whom NONE of the girls liked. A bitter boy.

I listened to message after hateful message, imagining each person in my mind as they spoke (except for the ones I didn't know who appeared in my mind as faceless people with big hair). Then I listened to them again. And again. It was my penance for spilling my guts. It turned out that the fifty-seven messages weren't from fifty-seven different people. Some had called more than once. Tyler had called four times. Serena six. I kept track in a notebook by my bed. The worst one had been from Jilly.

"You did it on purpose, didn't you? You wanted everyone to know how you felt about me. Well, you know what? I hate you, too." There was a pause, and I heard something like someone sucking in their breath and sniffling. "But who cares? That stuff you wrote makes you look way more stupid than I do." *Click.*

But there were a few rays of light in my dark, dark cave of despair. Like the pillow-kissing girl. And Ms. Moreno.

"There was a mix-up, Erin," she said. "After Tyler uploaded your files, I thought Mr. Arnett was checking them and he thought I was and then we had a number of problems come up that needed everyone's attention." She sighed heavily on the other end of the phone. "I suggested we wait to launch until after Thanksgiving so you could be here, too, but everyone was so ready to go. We tried to call you but no one picked up." Another pause. "I'm really sorry, Erin."

The other shining message was from Rosie: "Don't worry. It'll work out. I'll be over after school." I saved that one, too. But I kept going back to the others, replaying them over and over until Mom came back.

"What are you doing?" She rushed across my bedroom and pried the phone away from my ear. I was like a robot, pressing 3 to replay the message, 8 to save, # to skip to the next message. Even when the phone was out of my hand, my fingers kept moving to press the buttons.

"Oh, Erin."

I glanced up. The phone was pressed against her ear and Mom had tears in her eyes. I wondered vaguely which message she was listening to. She set the phone down and rubbed her temples. "Did you listen to all of them?"

I shrugged. Then I told her everything. About Mark, about Jilly, about Rosie, about Mark and Jilly, about Mark and Rosie, about Tyler and Serena (separately, not like they were a couple). She said, "Oh, Erin" about fifty-seven times and I couldn't tell if it was an I-can't-believe-you-would-write-such-things "Oh, Erin" or an I-really-feel-for-you "Oh, Erin."

"I'm Harriet in *Harriet the Spy,*" I wailed as Mom sat down on the end of my bed. In that book, Harriet had written nasty things about some of the kids she knew, including her two best friends. And they found her notebook and read all these horrible things about themselves. And then they hated her and wouldn't talk to her.

"No, you're not," Mom said. We had read the book together when

I was in fourth grade, then again in fifth. She loved it as much as I did. "First of all, you didn't spy on anyone. Second, Harriet doesn't tell her mom why she feels bad. Third, she goes and talks to the nice man with all the games —"

"The therapist," I interrupted.

Mom looked startled. "Well, yes. That's what he was. I didn't think you knew that."

"Carla's mom is in therapy," I said. When Mom looked puzzled I added, "She's my locker partner and was the peas in the Vegetable Medley."

Mom nodded. "Fourth, they finally found out Harriet was missing Ole Golly." Reaching out, she squeezed my shoulder and attempted a smile. "You told us everything so you won't have to go to therapy and we don't have a housekeeper. So you see? You're not Harriet at all."

I looked up at her, then down at my cast. "I have to transfer to a different school."

"Harriet went back to school," Mom said. "Remember? And all of her friends forgave her in the end."

"That's a book," I said. "It's not real life. It's not my life."

"Exactly," Mom said. "Things will turn out differently for you."

"Are you saying no one will forgive me in the end?"

"No." Mom sighed. One of those humongous ones that meant she felt really bad for me. "I'm saying you're different from Harriet, your friends are different from Janie and Sport, and you're not nearly as angry as Harriet. You expressed your feelings and everyone has a right to do that. It's just unfortunate that your feelings were made public."

I groaned loudly. I'd stayed awake most of the night going over everything I'd written in my blog. "The worst part is that I wrote a lot of that stuff weeks ago. I don't even feel that way anymore. Even about Serena."

"Really?" Mom raised an eyebrow.

"Yeah. I'd change it to the S.W. Dislike-o-Rama."

"Oh, Erin," she said, but she smiled. "Well, we've got four days of the break to figure out what to do. Then you'll go back to school on Monday and face all this."

I stared at her. How could she possibly make me go back after this?

"In the meantime," Mom continued, ignoring my look, "why don't you try to get some rest? We've got fifteen relatives showing up tomorrow for Thanksgiving dinner. I'm sure all the cousins will want to sign your cast." She patted my arm and left.

Throwing myself backward onto my pillows, I stared up at the ceiling. I was never, ever going back to Molly Brown Middle School. No way. And my parents couldn't make me, not in a million, trillion years. And there was no way I was going to be able to fall asleep. I was living a nightmare. How could I possibly sleep?

chapter 23

Erin Swift, aka Loser

"Are you INSANE?"

My bedroom door banged open and I sat upright in bed, my heart pounding like crazy. Sunlight streamed in my window so I knew it was still daytime.

"Wake up!" shouted Chris, barreling toward me. I raised my arms to ward off an attack but he stopped next to the bed, his hands clenched at his sides.

"What's your problem?" I said, sitting up and lowering my arms. I rested my cast on my lap, making sure he remembered his sister was injured and therefore should be treated delicately.

Too bad "delicate" wasn't anywhere in my brother's vicinity. "My problem? Do you want to know what my problem is?"

"Actually, no," I said, seeing his blazing eyes. "I changed my mind."

"Too late," Chris said, grabbing me by the shoulders. "Do you have any idea how much trouble you have caused? Do you?"

I glanced quickly up at him and then away. Oh, no. I hadn't written just about people at my school. I'd written about Chris, too. Serena must have called her sister at the high school. Stupid cell phones.

"You said you felt sorry for me," Chris snapped. "It was bad enough that you broadcast the fact that I liked — and I mean LIKED in the PAST tense — Amanda. That we saw her kissing Chad but to say you felt SORRY for me?" His fingers tightened on my arms. "The entire school now knows I wear frog underwear."

"With those baggy lowrider pants, they probably already knew." I tried to smile.

"That's not the point. You wrote it down. And you said I was drunk on Halloween. If Mom and Dad find out —"

"I said I thought you might be drunk, I —"

Chris continued as if I hadn't said anything. "And that stuff about the pictures? All these girls kept handing me their photos, asking me if I'd —" He squeezed my arms tighter and put his nose to mine. "God, I could kill you." I winced. He must have realized what he was doing because he pushed me back roughly. I smacked my head on the headboard.

"Ow," I said, rubbing the back of my head.

"You don't know what pain is, Puppet Girl."

I stared at him, unable to speak. Except for that first time when he got really mad, Chris had never said a word about the PI, and he'd never called me that name. Tears pricked my eyes, but I refused to blink. They would fall if I blinked.

"There," he said quietly. "Now maybe you're getting a little closer to knowing." He stormed out, slamming the door behind him. I stared at the closed door, trembling, my lip quivering as the tears rolled down my cheeks.

Wiping my sleeve across my eyes, I glanced down at my nightstand. A note was propped against my water glass. My hand shaking, I reached out to pick it up.

Erin (Not Harriet),
This is going to work out. I PROMISE! I'm downstairs in my office if you need me.

Hope you slept well.

I love you,

Mom

Poor Mom. She had no idea how truly horrible the situation was. How there was no way in the entire universe that it would work out. I'd lost my best friend, practically the entire school hated me, and now my brother hated me. Again.

The doorbell rang downstairs. A few seconds later I heard footsteps, then a soft knock at my door. "Erin? You awake?" Mom's voice. She must not have heard Chris storming around slamming doors, waking me up.

"Yeah," I said. "Come on in." My hand clenched the covers as the door swung open.

"Hey." Rosie stood next to my mom. "Did you get my message?"

I nodded and waved her in. "But I think you're a bit optimistic. I had fifty-seven voice mails. Most of them were hate voice mails."

"I'm sorry." Rosie sat in the chair at my desk.

"Are you only here because I didn't say anything mean about you on my website?"

Rosie laughed. "You did say I might be stuck up."

"But then I said you weren't."

"True," Rosie said. "But it doesn't matter. I know I'm not." She tugged on her braid. "Hmm, am I here because you didn't slam me like everyone else? I honestly don't know. I'd like to think I would be here even if you had said something mean about me, but I can't say for sure."

"At least you're honest."

Rosie smiled and sat down on the edge of my bed. "So, how are you doing?" She frowned. "I guess that's a dumb question."

I tossed the covers off and stood up, rubbing my cast. "How could this happen?"

Rosie shook her head. "Like Ms. Moreno said, there was a big mix-up. We didn't even get to do anything with your disc last night because everything went wacko. Ms. Moreno had to deal with a server problem and then Tyler forgot to tell Mr. Arnett because he helped Eric format his last page and then things got really crazy.

"Then this morning, the group that Serena is in lost one of their graphic files and we were all trying to find something else to use. And then Mark's column disappeared, then suddenly reappeared, and then Steve had gotten funny and added things like 'Janitorial Makeout' to the event listings, so we had to go through all of those and take out the joke ones."

Rosie looked at me. "Once all those things were solved, we just published it. I voted to wait for you, but most people wanted to go for it, so we did." She sighed. "We tried to call first thing, before . . ."

"I know."

Rosie threw her arm over the back of the chair. "We heard about it about ten after nine and Ms. Moreno shut the whole Intranet down, but not before someone had printed out your stuff and passed it around."

I collapsed on the floor, putting my head in the hand without the cast. "It's a nightmare. It's worse, way worse, than the PI."

"PI?" Rosie asked.

"The Puppet Incident."

"Oh. Yeah." Rosie had never said anything about that, and I was grateful to her.

"You think it's worse, too, don't you?"

"Well, a lot more people are involved, that's for sure," Rosie said.

"Jilly thinks I did it on purpose. To get back at her."

Rosie snorted. "That's crazy." She leaned toward me, touching my arm. "Erin, if I was working until midnight three nights in a row, I might accidentally switch some discs, too." She flopped down on the floor next to me. "She's just thinking about herself."

I glanced at Rosie. "She's not always like that, you know."

"I know," Rosie said. "You wouldn't be friends with her if she was."

I sighed. "I'm not friends with her right now."

"You will be," Rosie said. "Don't worry." She picked up my cast. "Looks a little bare, doesn't it?" She signed it: "To the best corny friend in the world."

I laughed but stopped because it felt strange, then laughed again. We sat in silence for a few moments, giggling every few seconds before sighing.

There was a knock at my door.

"Yeah?"

Mom poked her head in. "Do you girls want anything? Lemonade? Popcorn?"

"Yeah," we both said together. And laughed again.

Mom smiled. "Lemonade and popcorn coming up."

I glanced at Rosie. "You know she feels bad if she's letting me eat in my room."

We smiled at each other and then I frowned, leaning back against the bed.

"Did Mark read all the stuff I said about him?"

Rosie nodded. "Well, kind of. He read some, but he was so embarrassed he stopped reading. But other people told him about it."

"I'm SO embarrassed. Is he, like, freaking out about it? Is he totally mad at me?"

Rosie shook her head. "No. Just really embarrassed. Everyone's calling him Cute Boy. And I mean *everyone.*"

"It's better than Puppet Girl or Pinocchio." I flopped down on my bed. "That's probably why he didn't call."

"Pretty much," Rosie said.

"And I know Tyler and Serena are mad."

"She cried."

I sat up. "What?"

"At first she was furious, and then when everyone started saying stuff to her about the Hate-o-Rama, she ran into the bathroom and started crying. Her mascara was running and everything."

I shook my head. I had made Serena Poopendena cry. After all these years of torture and torment, I, Erin Penelope Swift, had reduced her to tears.

I felt like the biggest loser in the world.

chapter 24

The Gates of Heck

I was walking on death row. ETM&D (Evil Torture Mom and Dad) had refused my request to transfer to another school, even when I offered to eat all of my veggies, clean my room without being told, clean ALL the bathrooms including the toilets, and never ask for another thing as long as I lived.

"You need to go back," my dad said. I needed to shrivel up and disappear, but that didn't seem to be happening either. Mom had offered to take me to school so I wouldn't have to ride on the bus, but I said no. Her lame attempt at charity came too little, too late. Besides, if I had to go, I was going to do it full force. If she drove me it would look like I couldn't handle it, like I was avoiding everyone, especially Jilly. No, I would face it head-on. Right away.

I dragged my feet toward the bus stop, my arms wrapped around me to keep warm in the chilly November air. I wondered if there was any possibility that a four-day break and too much turkey and stuffing would make people forget. Or maybe a couple would be caught making out in Puppet Porter's office or something.

Dream on, Erin.

When I turned onto the street where the bus picked up, I saw Jilly coming from her street. My heart raced, flipped, twisted, practically choking me. In twenty more steps we would be only a few feet away from each other.

"Jilly." I said it quietly, even though no one else was there yet.

Jilly stood with her gloved hands clasped together in front of her, looking down the street. I could see how tight her jaw was, her teeth clenched so she had a bulge near the back of her cheek. She didn't seem to notice that I now wore a cast because I'd nearly broken a bone.

"Um, Jilly?"

"God," she said, wrapping her arms around herself. "When is this bus going to come?"

"I really need to talk to you." My voice was so small, I wasn't sure I'd spoken at all. But I knew I had when Jilly whirled to face me.

"Don't you think you've said enough? Don't you think you've hurt enough people by talking?"

"It was private!" I protested. "No one was supposed to see it. And I don't —"

"It doesn't matter if you didn't want anyone to see it! You said you hated me. Hated me, Erin! And you think I'm selfish and stuck up and a big baby. You wanted to strangle me, then decided to just put a muzzle on me." Her eyes blazed as she stepped toward me. "You said I had small boobs. Do you have any idea how embarrassing that is? Can you imagine how many people were looking at my chest all day long? Do you know how many Mounds bars I got last Wednesday? The vending machine ran out of them." Her voice was high and I knew she was trying not to cry. "I thought you were my friend, Erin. But you're just a big fat hypocrite!" She stomped a few feet away from me, but I saw tears spring to her eyes.

"I also said you were my best friend and I couldn't believe you wanted me for a friend. And you made me pick between the two of you. What was that about?"

"We're not talking about that right now, Erin. We're talking about you writing mean and hateful things for the entire school to see."

My breath was coming fast, my heart pounding. "You're right. I'm sorry. I didn't mean —"

"Hey! There she is!" Two eighth-grade boys sauntered up, one of them pointing at me. "You're the one who wrote all the stuff on the website," he said, then shook his hips. "Am I a hot tamale?" He made kissing noises, then turned to his friend. "Got a pillow? I want to make out." They both cracked up, leaning against each other for support.

My whole body tensed and I bit my lip to keep from crying.

The other one came over and put his face close to mine. "Where's Cute Boy? Has he declared his undying love?" He raised his arm. "Will you sniff under my arms to check for BO?" Then he turned to Jilly. "And isn't this your best friend that you HATE?"

Jilly's back stiffened.

"Shut up!" I shouted. "Just SHUT UP!"

I took off running down the block just as the bus turned the corner and headed for our stop. I didn't stop running until I was four blocks away, had turned three more corners, and was standing safely in front of the RV parked on the side of our neighbor's house. They usually drove it down to Texas at this time of the year, but something had come up so they were staying home. I bent down and felt under the rim of the motor home until my fingers located the hide-a-key. I'd seen them get the key out several times when they would get the RV ready for a trip. I looked all around before slipping inside, closing the door behind me.

The RV was cold and quiet. In front of me was the kitchen, a small square of tile with a sink, a stove, and about a foot of counter space. To my right, behind the driver and passenger seats, was a table tucked between two cushioned benches, like a booth in a restaurant. Across from it stood a couch. Above the cab was a bed. To my left was the bathroom and a bedroom, just a mattress and two pillows, without any bedding.

I wrapped my arms around me, shivering on a small rug. DEFCON 0. Even Chris didn't know about this and it was the first time I'd used it. I pulled off my backpack and slid into the booth, resting my hands on the table. I hadn't planned for this. I had no food, except one emergency Snickers and an old Tootsie Pop I'd started carrying around since my conversation with Mr. Foslowski. I had no books. No games. No paper. Nothing to do.

After what seemed like years, I stood up and crept to the window that faced our house. I was just feet away from where I had started this morning and yet it felt like miles. I knew my mom was inside our warm house, working on her latest client's website down in her basement office. Hmm. Maybe I could sneak in and get some books and some food. Warm up a little. No. Too risky. She was always popping upstairs, especially if a client called. She used that time to tidy up while she talked.

I let the curtain drop and turned around. I'd just have to stay here until 3:45, when I could safely walk in the door and tell her how I'd survived the whole BN (Blog Nightmare).

Sighing, I rummaged through the cupboards, looking for something to eat or read. I found a mystery novel under the front passenger seat and a box of crackers in the cupboard near the sink. Two blankets were stashed in a drawer under the bed and I pulled them out, wrapping them around me as I settled back into the booth.

At 8:35 by the dashboard clock, I heard our garage door go up. I ran to the window and peeked through the curtains as our car backed quickly down the driveway. Mom put the car into drive and sped down the street. Gee, she was in a hurry. But what a lucky break. After watching the car turn at the end of the block, I ran out of the RV and got a bunch of supplies from the house and used the bathroom. Then I ran back. Who knew where Mom had gone or when she'd be back?

It took me four hours to read two hundred pages and devour the box of crackers. A quick check of the dashboard clock told me it was noon. Three hours and forty-five minutes to go. And I mean GO. I needed to pee again. I wondered if it was okay to use the bathroom in the RV. I decided I'd better hold it. I could do it. Didn't I go all night without peeing?

Sleep. That would get my mind off my bladder. I grabbed the blankets and climbed up on the mattress at the back of the RV.

• • •

When I woke up, I hurried to check the time. Three thirty-nine! Wow. I'd done it. I was cold and stiff but I'd made it through my first day back at school without going back to school.

I quickly put everything back the way it had been, including the empty box of crackers. Then I grabbed my backpack and the key and hustled out the door.

Both of my parents were pacing around the living room when I came in. They turned to look at me at the same time, their faces registering relief and anger.

"Where have you been?" My dad strode over and grabbed me by the shoulders.

"I —"

"The school called first thing this morning, wondering why we hadn't called in your absence," my mom said. "Your dad and I have been looking everywhere for you."

"You weren't at the tree house," Chris said. "Or anywhere else that I knew to look."

It was Chris's face that did me in, scared and a little lost. I burst into tears and threw myself into my dad's arms, sobbing out everything that had happened at the bus stop. "I couldn't go to school," I gasped between sniffles and sobs. "I just couldn't. There were only three people at the bus stop and they all hated me. I couldn't face an entire school."

"Shh, shh," my dad said, stroking my head. "It's going to be okay."

Chris walked over and dropped a hand on my shoulder. "I got a copy of the Intranet thing and read it," he said. "You know way more pain than I ever will."

Well, of course it was circulating around the high school. My misery knew no end.

Chris punched my arm lightly. "You'll get through it."

I sighed heavily. I could picture myself walking down the hallways of MBMS tomorrow, every set of eyes on me . . . AGAIN. For being mean and baring my lovesick soul. I would rather walk on hot coals in bare feet. Or be banned from the computer forever, as hard as that would be. Or even stop eating Snickers for the rest of my life.

"Can't I stay home one more day?" I pleaded. "Just one more?"

My parents exchanged looks. I could see the pain in their eyes. Maybe they did remember what it was like to be twelve. "I have to say there's a part of me that wants to let you," Mom said. "When I was in fifth grade, Tommy Gerardi poured blue paint over my head. It didn't come out for a week. They called me Little Girl Blue every day."

"That's why we weren't allowed to paint the family room blue," my dad added. Mom smacked him playfully.

"Anyway, I can't know exactly how you're feeling, Erin," Mom continued. "But I can imagine how difficult it will be at school. And I wish I could protect you from it. But I know that isn't the right answer. You can't hide from your problems forever."

"I don't want to hide forever," I said. "Just tomorrow. And maybe the next day."

My dad smiled. "You'll get through this, Erin," he said. "You're stronger than you think."

Deluded parents were worse than not understanding parents. What would they do when they found out I was the biggest weakling to walk on two large feet?

chapter 25

Erin Swift and the Chamber of Horrors

I timed my arrival at the bus stop so it would coincide with the arrival of the bus, holding back until the boys from our stop were already on. Jilly wasn't there. No doubt she had gotten a ride to school so she wouldn't have to deal with me. I took the first available seat and kept my eyes straight ahead. Several kids said things about my blog, then said things about Jilly. At the next stop, Rosie got on and sat with me. That gave me courage. I stood up and turned around. "I'm the one who wrote the stuff, not her," I said. "I was mad at her, okay? Just leave her out of it." I plopped back down in my seat. Rosie smiled and squeezed my wrist. There were a few moments of silence, and then they all started asking about Cute Boy and when would they get their Snickers because they'd clicked on SNICKERS.

I looked at my watch. Seven fifty-five. Only seven hours and twenty-five minutes to go.

. . .

8:35 A.M. Homeroom. Serena gave me a look that burned a hole through my head. I took two steps toward her, but she got up and moved to the other side of the room. "Don't even think about coming anywhere near me, Erin Swift." All the kids stared at me and I couldn't breathe. Ms. Archer motioned me to the front of the room.

"This whole thing is quite . . . tragic," she said.

I nodded. I hoped she wouldn't compare it to one of the Shakespeare plays she was threatening to make us read.

"It'll work out, Erin. Don't you worry."

All the grown-ups in my life seemed to be living in some kind of "everything works out" fantasy world. They had no idea what it was like on the other side, the reality side.

"Thanks, Ms. Archer. I hope so."

I sat in my seat behind Mark and tried to ignore the eyes on me, the ones that always looked quickly away the minute I tried to make eye contact.

I couldn't even look at Mark's head in front of me. My cheeks felt like they were on fire. Mark had read all that stuff I wrote about him. I knew I might die of embarrassment right in my seat. I begged the chair to collapse, for a hole to open up in the floor and me to sink into it, never to be seen again. Rosie smiled encouragingly at me, the only one who would actually return my gaze, but it didn't help. The world had shut the door on me. I was on the outside.

9:18 A.M. English. I managed to survive the halls. Everyone was talking about the blog and my site. I saw Carla and she gave me a sad smile, which was almost worse than no smile. I kept my head down and wished myself invisible, which is hard when your feet are so very visible.

10:25 A.M. Word processing class. Ms. Moreno pulled me aside.

"I'm so sorry this happened, Erin," she said. "I meant to look, I really did. But then . . . well, things got crazy." She squeezed my shoulders. "I really wished I pushed harder to wait until after Thanksgiving break to launch, because you were so much a part of this. But the students were so eager to see it and the kids in the Club had everything ready . . ." Her voice trailed off and I could see real pain in her eyes. "If only we'd waited."

"It's okay," I said, even though it most obviously wasn't. I took my seat.

When the bell rang, I got up and pulled my backpack off my chair, nearly bumping into Mark trying to get down the aisle.

"Sorry," we both said. He looked at me and quickly looked away. It was so awkward I thought I would burst into tears. As if he had seen me naked and was trying not to look at my private parts. I had an urge to cover my chest or put a big leaf over the front of my jeans like I'd seen in a picture of Adam and Eve. But I knew it wouldn't help. He turned and practically ran from the room.

As I headed down the hall, someone tugged on my sleeve. "Um, Erin?" A girl's voice. "Erin, I just wanted to thank you for writing some of those things."

Huh? I turned around to see if she was making fun of me, about to come in for the kill. But her expression was sincere.

"I guess that sounds kind of weird, but I've had a lot of the same feelings about boys." She leaned over and whispered, "I've kissed my pillow, too."

I looked at her, surprised. "You're the one?"

The girl nodded. "I'm sorry I hung up. I was just, well, embarrassed." She smiled shyly. "But I'm glad I'm not the only one."

"Maybe we'll start a club," I said. "The Pillow Kissers Club."

She giggled and I smiled. Maybe this wouldn't be so horrible after all.

11:45 A.M. I made it to lunch. Rosie sat with me, a gesture that assures her a top seat in heaven if I have anything to say about it, which I don't. People were still making comments. Most of them were making fun of me and my "tell-all blog," or told me I was mean and spiteful for writing things about Serena and Jilly. But a few came up and said surprising things.

"You have a way of saying things," one boy said. "You made me laugh." Then he looked serious. "When are you going to put up Serena's virtual dartboard?"

Another girl said that her sister had a crush on my brother and had gone out and bought a pair of froggy boxers.

"She doesn't think he's weird?"

The girl shook her head. "After what you wrote, she thinks he's smart and sensitive."

Rosie smiled at me. "See? It's not all bad."

But most of it was. I had to hold on to these small life-preserver comments in a sea of smart remarks about pillow kissing, hot tamales, and sniffing BO.

3:10 p.m. Last bell. I ran down the hall, nearly crashing into Mr. Foslowski.

"Whoa, there, girl. What's your hurry?" He stepped back and his face changed. "Ah. My little stowaway." He nodded his head. "Looks like you got yourself into a little more trouble, eh?"

"A little?"

Mr. Foslowski smiled. "Got any Tootsie Pops?"

"What?" I could not think about candy at a time like this.

"Tootsie Pops? Do you have any?"

I furrowed my brow but reached in my backpack. "I've got one. But it's kind of old." Mr. Foslowski held up his hand to stop me.

"I'm glad you've got one," he said. "Here's another." He held out a grape Tootsie. "Now you have two."

I looked at him, thinking he might need professional help. Like candy was going to help me with the BN. "Thanks," I said, sliding it into my pocket. "I've got to go to the lab."

"Don't bite it," Mr. Foslowski called after me.

• • •

"This was, by far, the worst day of my life," I said to Rosie when she met me in the hall on the way to the computer lab. "Mark runs away whenever I'm around and Jilly won't return my calls. She doesn't even answer the phone anymore. It's always her mom or dad or voice mail." I felt bad about that. Jilly loved to answer the phone because it was almost always for her. But because of me she didn't get to do that anymore.

"Give her time," Rosie said.

"She won't even look at me," I said. "It's like I'm invisible."

Rosie sighed. "I'm sorry," she said. "But I'm glad you're coming to the lab."

"I'm not touching a keyboard or mouse," I said. "I've given up the computer for good. I'm only going to see if Tyler will talk to me." Jilly and Serena wouldn't let me apologize, but I was hoping Tyler would. When we got to the lab, I peered inside. Good. Mark wasn't there yet. I started toward Tyler, but he gave me the meanest Death Stare I'd ever seen. And when I tried to talk to him, he kept his eyes on his monitor. "Dorks don't talk to fake friends," he said.

Strike three.

chapter 26

Out of Fashion

I stood in front of my closet on Sunday afternoon, staring at the clothes hanging in a neat row. There weren't that many. Just a few fancy shirts Jilly had insisted I buy and some nice pants that couldn't be stuffed in a drawer without near-permanent damage. The rest were in my dresser.

In my other life, Jilly would be standing next to me, moving from closet to dresser as she selected and wrote down my wardrobe for the week.

In this life, I was alone.

"Need some help?" My mother stood at the doorway, watching me. I was getting tired of my family's looks of pity and compassion. It was hard enough losing my best friends; I didn't need my family feeling sorry for me.

"She's still mad," I said.

Mom stepped into the room. "Jilly has a good eye for fashion." She fingered a blue blouse Jilly had gotten me at the Limited. "She really knows what you look good in."

I glanced at Mom. I had started to think that maybe Jilly dressed me so I wouldn't embarrass her with my choice of clothes. But the minute Mom said that, I knew it was true. Jilly liked to look her best and liked to see me looking my best.

It was funny how many times I had wished she wouldn't be so pushy, telling me how to walk in mega spike heels, even how to laugh when you wanted someone to think you were having a great time when you really weren't. But right now I would have given anything for Jilly to be here, telling me what to wear.

"What do you want to wear?" Mom said softly. "What do you choose?"

I choose to turn back the clock, I wanted to say. To start all over. To never write in a blog or think any thoughts at all about anyone.

"It doesn't matter what I choose," I said. "Jilly's still not my friend."

• • •

As Christmas break loomed, the thought of spending it by myself (Rosie was going to Mexico to visit relatives) was overwhelmingly depressing. I knew I couldn't keep moping around. I had made a big, big mistake and I needed to do something to try to fix it.

I decided to launch Operation Apology Letter. I wrote each of my four victims a letter, apologizing and asking for forgiveness. I started with Serena's and ended with Jilly's, which was, by far, the hardest one to write. As I dropped each one in the mailbox at the end of our block, my heart beat a little faster. I held onto Jilly's the longest, wondering if I'd said everything I should have, left out things I didn't need to say. Finally, I let it slip through my fingers, closing the mailbox door so it slid down inside.

"It's a good start," my mother said when I got back. "I'm proud of you."

I tried to smile, but instead I started crying. Mom wrapped her arms around me.

"Don't say it's going to be okay," I sniffled. "Because it isn't."

"It might be," Mom said. She pulled a tissue from her purse and handed it to me. As I blew my nose, she held me close. "You're doing everything you can, Erin. The rest is up to them." She gave me a little squeeze. "People can surprise you," she said. "Let them."

• • •

I knew everyone would get their letter the next day. So I had to wait until Friday, the last day of school before the winter break, to see what they would do. When I arrived at my locker, three unopened envelopes were stuffed in the slats — the ones I'd sent Tyler, Serena, and Jilly. Mark's wasn't in my locker, but he did smile at me in homeroom this morning and asked me a question about formatting in word processing. I guess that was something.

"I wish you weren't going to be gone," I said to Rosie as we walked to the bus after school. I looked up as a brisk December wind picked up and a few snowflakes began falling. I stuck my tongue out and caught a flake.

"What are you going to do?" asked Rosie.

I shrugged. Ms. Moreno had asked if I would work on the Intranet over the break but I'd said no. I had to keep my punishment. No more computers.

"Well, my grandma always says, 'The hardest work is to do nothing.'"

"I wrote the letters," I said. "I don't know what else to do."

"I know." We climbed on the bus and my eyes scanned the seats. *Whew.* Jilly wasn't on yet. I wouldn't have to suffer her Death Stare. Rosie and I found seats over the wheel well because she liked to put her feet on it. As I stuffed my backpack on the floor in front of me, Jilly got on the bus and sat in front next to Bus Boy. I sucked in air and my heart pounded. But she didn't look back. Didn't even turn her head an inch. Which was good. Because I didn't want that horrible look she might give me. So it was good that she hadn't looked back. It was good that I was completely invisible.

"Erin, did you hear what I said?" Rosie poked her elbow into my arm. "We're launching the Intranet when we get back from Christmas break."

This got my attention. "You're launching?" Ms. Moreno and Mr. Arnett had suspended the Intranet indefinitely. The kids were still working on pages but really just for practice. No one had set a date.

"Yeah," said Rosie. "Give people time to, you know, kind of forget about the first launch."

I looked at her. I'd been so wrapped up in how the BN had affected me, I hadn't thought about what it meant to all the other kids who had worked so hard on the Intranet. "I'm sorry," I said. "I feel horrible."

Rosie nodded. "I know."

"Most of my blog was about my feelings, but everyone is focusing on what I said about other people." I shook my head. "I'm the one who should be absolutely mortified." That was a new word I'd learned and I liked it. It fit my situation much better than "embarrassed." "Actually, I *am* absolutely mortified."

"People always want to know the bad in other people, that's what my mom says. It's a way for them to feel better about themselves."

"Can't they feel better without making someone else feel bad?"

Rosie didn't say anything. She just looked at me. I didn't like how that look made me feel.

"I have reading to do," I said, leaning over to pull a book out of my backpack. We didn't say another word for the rest of the ride.

 **Thursday, December 12**

I know I said I'd never touch a computer again but I can't stand it. I promise I'll delete this entry as soon as I'm finished so it won't fall into the wrong hands, but I've got to do this.

Things That Totally Bum Me Out

Almost 2 weeks have passed and nothing has changed, except there was a little less chatter about my blog.

- Serena, Jilly, Tyler, and Mark are still not talking to me.

- Today I saw Jilly by the buses after school, talking to Bus Boy...doing most of the talking, surprise. Mark walked by and they didn't even look at each other. He stopped to talk to a friend and I just watched him for a minute...never noticed how the tip of his tongue stuck out a little when he had his mouth open...reminded me of a little kid...he looked kind of silly, actually. But I miss him.

- Mark and I haven't had a real conversation since the BN. I have no idea how he and Jilly broke up, since neither of them is really talking to me, or how it's affecting them. And even though I'm giving up the computer, Mark and I could still talk about it. And we could shoot hoops. And make fun of Puppet Porter.

It's like they are all people I saw in a movie once, a movie I watched over and over until it felt like it had happened to me.

But then the credits roll and I realize that I really didn't know the people in the movie at all, they weren't a part of my life.

When I look at Jilly, it's like she's on 1 side of a big canyon and I'm on the other...I don't see any way to get across to her. And even if I did, she's got her back to me on the other side so she wouldn't even know I was coming.

Things That Make Me Feel a Little Better (but not much)

- Ms. Moreno called me at home again, asking me to come back to I-Club. I told her no. She told me it was a terrible misunderstanding, a horrible mistake, but I didn't have to quit using computers.

But it's the punishment I've assigned myself and I plan to stick with it (right after I delete this page).

It kind of stinks, though, cuz so much of my life is about the computer. Computer games, helping my mom, designing my own website, and this blog.

Ok, More Things That Kind of Make Me Feel Better...

- Chris is being pretty nice to me.

- Rosie is still my friend.

Again I ask: Why does it seem like the things that totally bum me out are so much bigger than the things that make me feel better?

chapter 27

ATTENTION!

On Saturday, the first day of our winter break, I borrowed the neighbor's dog so I'd have an excuse to walk by Jilly's house. She never came out. I shuffled around the block and when I passed her house again, I thought I saw the curtains move in the living room but I wasn't sure.

On Sunday, I brought over some of the things she'd left at my house — two CDs, some fingernail polish, and some hair clips. I also brought a bottle of her favorite perfume, wrapped in a pretty box with a ribbon.

I was so nervous standing on her doorstep, I thought I'd either faint, puke, or both. My whole body shook. Would she see me? What would I say to her? I looked down at the cement, my eyes following the familiar crack that led from under the WELCOME mat all the way across to the other side of the porch. How many times had we traced it with chalk, or jumped over it so we wouldn't break our mother's back? Was it only four months ago that we were standing on this porch, holding those MBMS envelopes, wondering if we'd be together?

Mrs. Hennessey answered the door. "Jillian is upstairs," she whispered, as if the house were full of sleeping children. "I don't think she wants to be disturbed."

I sighed, feeling sad and relieved. I had no idea what I would have said to her.

"I'm really, really sorry," I said. I couldn't even look at Jilly's mom. But her fingers touched my chin gently, lifting my face.

"So am I, honey. So am I." Her eyes were kind and my lip quivered with gratitude. At least Jilly's mom didn't hate me. I wanted to ask her if she thought Jilly would ever forgive me, but I was afraid to.

"Is there a message?" Mrs. Hennessey asked.

I thought for a minute. "Tell her I have no idea what to wear."

• • •

Jilly and I had exchanged gifts on Christmas Eve every year since we were six or seven. It was hard to light the candles and sing songs with my family, watching the time click by, knowing there would be no guessing and giggling and ripping off ribbons and paper before opening what always seemed the perfect gift. I had bought her present months ago — a pair of faux pearl earrings that she'd admired — and it sat, looking small and sad in its bright foil wrapping, on my dresser.

The days over winter break seemed to drag on without end. It was December 26. Ten more days until school started up again. I wandered downstairs to Mom's office. Her desk was clean except for a series of papers with diagrams and markings indicating the flow of the website she was working on. A dark green vine wound its way across the top of the bookcase, which was filled with computer books, novels, and instruction guides.

"That's a cool intro," I said, leaning over her shoulder. She was designing a website for a silk plant company and had this beautiful image appearing and reappearing on the screen.

"I'm having trouble deciding how the slogan should appear," Mom said. "Should it slide in from one side or be a dissolve of some kind?"

With a few clicks she demonstrated the slide from the left.

"That's nice," I said, ignoring my twitching fingers, itching to grab the mouse. “What about a fade-in? I think that would look better since it’s just text.”

Mom made the selections and tested it. “Perfect,” she said. She smiled over her shoulder at me. “Thank you.”

I shrugged. It wasn’t much. I watched her for a few minutes longer, as if I might be able to find a clue in her design that would help me with my problem.

“I don’t know what to do,” I said softly.

“You can help me,” Mom said. When I didn’t move, she swiveled around in her chair and looked at me. “Oh,” she said when she saw my face. “Honey, what else can you do? You’ve called, you’ve written letters, you’ve apologized and asked for forgiveness over and over again. You’ve even sent gifts.” I’d sent a basketball T-shirt to Mark, a web design book to Tyler, a gift certificate to PacSun to Jilly, and one for the Gap to Serena. And I’d called most of them over and over again until their parents begged me to stop.

“You just have to let it take its course,” Mom said. “I know it’s hard, but that’s the way it has to be.”

I left her office and climbed the stairs to the main floor, sinking into the couch in the family room. TV. My new best friend. My arm itched beneath my cast so I reached for the knitting needle and poked. Sighing, I clicked the buttons on the TV remote.

Chris sat down in the chair next to the couch. I didn’t look at him. “I’m sorry you and Hennessey are still fighting. I kind of miss her bossing me around.”

I flicked my eyes to him, then back to the TV.

“You said some stuff about her, Erin. But she also walked out on your friendship. You can’t take the blame for the whole thing.”

“Did you see what I wrote about her?”

Chris nodded.

"The entire school saw that," I said. "The entire school read that I think she's a baby and I hate her." I didn't even get into the stuff about Mark. I was glad Chris hadn't made fun of me. Sighing, I flicked the channel again. "I even told her monster secret. I promised I would never tell anyone. She'll never forgive me."

"You just need to approach the whole thing in the right way."

"How? Mom says I need to let it run its course."

Chris shrugged. "Maybe she's right."

"But what if she isn't? What if there is something else I can do?"

Chris smiled at me. "Just do it."

I was about to reply when Chris leaned forward in his chair.

"Hey! Look at that guy!" He pointed to the TV, laughing. A man was wearing some kind of a sign that draped down his front and back. The front sign said, SAVE THE WHOOPING CRANE. The back sign said, GOING NUDE FOR NATURE.

"He's naked," Chris exclaimed. "Totally naked."

"It would be more effective if he were in the Necedah National Wildlife Refuge in Wisconsin in the freezing cold rather than where they migrate to Florida." My dad chuckled as he stepped into the room. "But that's one way to call attention to your cause."

I stared at my dad. Calling attention to my cause. I looked back at the TV. Maybe there was one last thing I could do about the whole BN.

chapter 28

Spam With a Purpose

Mom and Chris drove me to school on January 6 where I huddled in the back, clutching my sandwich board. My dad had told me what it was called when I showed my parents what I was doing. I planned to be what I termed "walking spam." I didn't plan to be naked, but I was wearing black stretch pants and a black turtleneck and had covered my cast in black tape. I wanted all the focus to be on my message.

I pushed the board away from me and read the front again:

TO:
JILLIAN G. HENNESSEY,
MARK SACKS,
SERENA WORTHINGTON,
AND
TYLER GALLEON
I'M SORRY!
I REALLY BLEW IT
AND I KNOW IT.
I HOPE SOMEDAY YOU WILL FORGIVE ME.
I'M GOING TO WEAR THIS SIGN UNTIL YOU DO.

On the back, the sign said:

STUDENTS OF MBMS:
PLEASE CHECK OUT
THE NEW AND IMPROVED
SCHOOL INTRANET!!!
COMMERCIAL-FREE INFORMATION
AND ENTERTAINMENT.
CHECK THE HOME PAGE TOMORROW
FOR AN IMPORTANT MESSAGE.

• • •

When we pulled up in front of MBMS, my heart did a triple back flip with a half twist. Maybe I should dive into the Forbidden Hedge and forget the whole thing. "I don't know if I can get out of the car."

"You don't have to do this, Erin," Mom said. "No one will know. You've said what you wanted to say on the home page. There's no need to wear the sandwich board."

I knew she was right. But I also knew I needed to do something big and crazy that was my choice, not something someone else did to me or I did by accident.

"You're either incredibly brave or incredibly stupid," Chris said. But he was smiling. He had come along to give me support, and I appreciated it.

"We'll see," I said. Taking a deep breath, I got out. Chris handed me the sandwich board. "Thanks for driving me," I said as I turned to face the building. "Here goes." I slammed the door shut, then pulled the straps over my head and adjusted the boards, front and back.

I heard the window roll down and turned. "Good luck, honey," Mom said. I could see concern in her eyes, but I just smiled and waved. After the PI and the BN, being a walking advertisement should be easy, right?

• • •

I thought I'd be used to the stares. After all, people had stared at me after the PI, and had stared some more when I came back after the BN. But it was still weird to have heads turn, eyes drop down to read the words. Some people smiled. Some rolled their eyes. I just walked on.

"You are something else," Mr. Foslowski said when he saw me. "You still got those Tootsie Pops I gave you?"

I nodded.

"Good. You'll need 'em."

I shook my head and kept going.

When I stepped into homeroom, I stopped inside the door, making sure I was facing Serena. She glanced up, looked startled, then read the front. I turned around so she could read the back. Then I faced her again.

"I hope you can keep it looking that good for prom when you're a senior in high school," Serena said. "Because that's how long you'll be wearing it."

My heart sank. I hadn't expected everything to be great right away, but I guess I wasn't ready for Serena. Mustering up my courage, I smiled at her.

"I guess I'd better keep it clean, then."

She looked a little surprised, then quickly turned away.

I found out right away that I couldn't sit down in the sandwich board.

"What should I do?" I asked Rosie. "I promised to wear it all the time."

"I don't think people expect you to wear it all the time. What if you have to go to the bathroom?"

"That's true," I said. I took it off and set it up near the front of the classroom with the backside turned out.

This continued for the rest of the morning. I wore the sandwich board everywhere I went, taking it off only to sit down or go to the bathroom. But it was always in sight. When Rosie and I got to the cafeteria for lunch, I scanned the room for Tyler. It took me awhile to spot him because his hair wasn't spiky. Instead, it fell in soft brown waves around his face.

"He sure looks different," I said, before walking over to him. His eyes got bigger and bigger as he read the sign.

"Hey, Tyler. Your name's on that," said one of his friends.

"Check out the MBMS Intranet tomorrow," I said, turning to leave.

"Wait." Tyler's voice stopped me. I bit my lip and turned around to face him.

"Yeah?"

"I'm sorry about what I said the first day of I-Club. About learning from Big Foot." He leaned forward and whispered in my ear. "And the mean poem on your voice mail."

"It's okay," I said. "I'm sorry about calling you dorky. You're really not. I would have changed my pages a long time ago if I thought anyone would see it." I smiled. "Read my letter on the Intranet tomorrow. Okay?"

"Okay," he said.

"What did you do to your hair?"

"It's what he didn't do," said one of his friends, rubbing Tyler's head and laughing. "For you."

"Shut up," Tyler said, slugging the boy in the shoulder.

"You should wear your hair the way you like it," I said before turning away.

. . .

Jilly was alone at her locker, something that rarely happened when I used to meet her there. I put my hand over my beating heart, took a breath, and walked down the hallway, stopping about a foot from her.

"I wondered when I'd see you," she said, not looking at me or the sign.

I didn't say anything. I wanted her to react to the sign, to see how I was calling attention to my cause. To see me walking in it. For her.

Jilly rummaged in her locker for what seemed an eternity. The straps on my shoulders dug into my skin and I shifted my weight.

"I hope that's comfortable," she said, pulling out her books and closing the locker.

I swallowed. "It'd better be. Serena said I'll be wearing it to my Senior Prom."

Jilly laughed out loud. "And I thought making you wear it all week would be too much."

I smiled. "Read my letter tomorrow, okay? Then, if you still can't forgive me, I'll stop trying. I'll keep wearing the sign, but I'll stop trying to be your friend anymore."

"I'll read it," Jilly said. Then she stepped around me and waved at someone behind me. I looked over my shoulder and saw Bus Boy. I guessed they were an item now. It was strange to think that Jilly's life was going on without me and I didn't have a blow-by-blow account. It made me sad.

I stuck the sandwich board in Mr. Foslowski's closet the way we'd arranged and headed for the bus. The only thing left was to see how everyone reacted to my letter.

Negative words had gotten me into this mess. I sure hoped positive ones could get me out.

Tuesday, January 7

Dear students of Molly Brown Middle School,

My name is Erin Swift. Those of you who have been here since the beginning may know me as Pinocchio or Puppet Girl. Or the girl who trips over her big feet.

But I guess that now, most of you know me as the person who wrote some very personal things about my life and some people at this school in my own private blog and web pages, which got out on the school Intranet by mistake.

I'm completely MORTIFIED about how much people know about my feelings. But worse than that is knowing that I've hurt some people and that some of you have hurt them, 2, because of things I wrote.

First of all, to Serena Worthington. I've known you since kindergarten and we've never really gotten along. You've picked on me, cut my hair, made fun of me, and have been pretty mean. But what I said on my web page about you was really bad. I was so mad at you for the stuff that happened that I just wasn't thinking. The thing is, since working on the MBMS Intranet together, I don't hate you anymore. You have some really good ideas and when you're not being snotty, you're actually sort of nice. I wish I had taken off that page about you because it isn't true anymore. But I didn't take it off and lots of people saw it and I'm really sorry. I hope 1 day you'll forgive me instead of getting revenge like you have before. I'm not sure how much more humiliation I can take.

Second, to Mark Sacks, there isn't a lot to say that a zillion kids didn't read on my pages. I'm sorry I embarrassed you so much. This really smart guy said that good friends are like Tootsie Pops, they last a long time if you don't bite them. I bit into this 1 and I'm sorry. I hope 1 day we can be friends again.

Third, to Tyler Galleon, the most non-dorky boy in the entire school. You really worked hard on the Intranet and were always doing things to help out. You've been my friend this whole time and I didn't even know it. I really blew it with you and I'm sorry.

Finally, to Jillian Gail Hennessey, who has been my best friend since kindergarten. I'm jealous of you. There, I said it. People always love you, even though you can be a little bossy. You always seem to get what you want and sometimes I feel like nobody next to you. But that's my problem, not yours. We definitely have a lot to talk about and I hope we get a chance to do it. I'm really, REALLY, REALLY sorry, Jilly. I know I took a pretty big bite out of the Tootsie Pop, but I think there might be something left inside. I hope you do, 2.

I also want to thank Rosie Velarde, who has stood beside me when nobody else did. She really knows what it means to be a friend. That's one special Tootsie Pop.

If I had a do over and could change things...honestly, I'm not sure I would. I know that sounds crazy but it's true. I learned a lot about myself, a lot about friendship, and a lot about going to the bathroom wearing a sandwich board. :-)

I hope some of you will stop me in the hall and say hi. I'll be the 1 wearing the sandwich board until the Senior Prom and beyond.

Thanks for listening.

Sincerely,
Erin Penelope Swift

P.S. Cherry Tootsies are my favorite. 

chapter 29

TSR (Terminate and Stay Resident)

There were exactly ten cherry Tootsie Pops stuck in my locker when I came to it at the end of the day. Well, it wasn't a zillion like Jilly would have gotten, but it was a start. Lots of people stopped me to say hi, most of them asking if any of the four had forgiven me yet.

"Two so far," I told the last person who had asked. One of the Tootsie Pops was from Mark, who had attached a note saying, "Cherry's my favorite, too." Tyler had come up to me after class, blushed, and thanked me for what I said in the online letter. His hair was spiky again.

"I like it," I had said, pointing to his head. "It's you."

"Yeah," he said, grinning. "It is."

I pulled the sandwich board over my head and walked down the hall.

"Well, well, well," Mr. Foslowski said. "Things are going to seem mighty quiet around here if you stop making so many mistakes."

"Quiet is good," I said. "Really good." I held out the boards. "Can you take these?"

"Sure. But I don't think you'll have to wear them much longer."

"Only two down," I said. "The boys. Two to go." *And they won't be easy,* I thought.

"Oh, I have a feeling they'll come around. Especially Jilly."

"That still leaves Serena."

"The one involved in the Puppet Caper?"

I nodded.

"Her, too."

I snorted. "You don't know Serena Worthington."

. . .

It turned out, neither did I. While I was heading to the custodian's closet to store the sandwich board on Thursday, she came up to me and said, "Oh, all right. Enough already. Take that stupid thing off before I die of embarrassment."

"You?"

"Yes," Serena said, wrinkling her nose as if she really couldn't believe she was saying it. "I'm the holdout. People know that everyone has forgiven you except me so they'll know you're still wearing it because of me. I'm getting all these looks like I'm some kind of torture lady or something. So just take it off, will you?"

"Jilly hasn't forgiven me either," I said.

"She hasn't?" I could see Serena's mind working with this information. After she processed it, she smiled. "Good. Then I'm not last. Take it off. And don't leave it out where people can see it." She waved it away like an annoying fly.

"But I need to wear it for Jilly tomorrow."

Serena frowned. "Well, then put something on it that says I told you to take it off. People need to know that."

I knew this was as good as I was going to get with Serena.

"Okay," I said. "I will."

"I hope Jilly hurries up. The sooner people forget about it, the better."

"Definitely," I said. I pulled out a permanent marker and wrote "Serena told me to take this off" next to her name. Then I slipped it into the janitor's closet before turning back toward my locker.

“So, I’ll see you at the Intranet Club, right?” Serena crossed her arms and tapped her foot.

I stared at her.

“Right?” she said again.

“Right,” I said, barely able to get the word out. Disbelief can, indeed, render one speechless.

chapter 30

Home Page Advantage

When I got home from school that afternoon, there was a message from Mark asking me to meet him at the Y to shoot baskets.

I was surprised my heart didn't do any fancy gymnastics when I heard his voice. I guessed all the excitement had cleared all of my emotions out of me.

. . .

The gym was pretty packed when I arrived. Mark stood at a far basket, shooting free throws. I walked around the perimeter of the court, dodging wayward balls along the way. He passed the ball to me when I got close and we played a couple of games of one-on-one. I won both this time.

"Meet me on the soccer field," I said, leaning over and putting my hands on my knees to catch my breath. "The torture will continue."

He laughed and faked like he was throwing the ball at my face. I ducked. We shot a bunch of free throws, then headed for the vending machines in the hall. After snagging some Gatorades, we sat on the floor near the gym, gulping quickly as athletic footwear shuffled by.

"So, things seem to be turning out okay." Mark didn't look at me when he said it, just took another long drink.

"Yeah. I got lucky I guess." I didn't say I still had another semester to go. I might jinx it.

"You said some nice stuff. And you meant it." He wiped his mouth with the back of his hand. "Thanks for the letter. You know. The one you mailed to me. And the stuff you said on the Intranet."

"The letter to the student body?"

"Yeah. That stuff."

My stomach clutched. I hoped he wasn't going to bring up the stuff I wrote about him in my blog.

"So, that other stuff you wrote in that thing. Your online journal or whatever."

Shoot. He was.

"What about it?" I took a drink, hoping he didn't notice how shaky my hand was.

"Did you mean it all?"

"What?"

"The stuff you said."

"About what?"

"Gee, Erin. Do I have to just say it?" His face was bright red and he wiped his sweaty forehead with the bottom of his T-shirt.

"Yes, because I don't know what you're talking about." I knew exactly what he was talking about, but I was enjoying his discomfort. I had had way more pain about this than he did.

"That stuff about you liking me. You know. More than a friend." He let out a big breath, as if he'd just told a secret he'd been holding inside for years.

"Did I mean it?" I asked. He nodded. "Yeah. I did. When I wrote it."

His face fell a little. "You mean you don't anymore."

"I don't think so. Why?"

"Oh. Well, that's good."

"It is?"

"Yeah."

"Oh." Boy, were we master conversationalists or what? Actually we were. As long as the topic didn't involve anything deep like. I decided to take the plunge into enemy territory. "I'm sorry about Jilly."

Mark shrugged. "I think we both stopped liking each other at the same time. It's just weird being around her now." He glanced at me and took another swig of Gatorade. "You were kind of right about her, Erin. She does talk a lot about herself."

I smiled. "She's got a good heart underneath all that gabbing."

"I guess." Mark turned to look down the hall. "I'm glad we're friends."

"Me, too."

We were quiet for several moments, the only sound the *squeak-squeak* of shoes and the echoing *smack-smack* of basketballs on the court down the hall.

"And I'm glad you decided to come back to I-Club," Mark said. "It wasn't the same without you."

"Really?"

"Really," Mark said. "I had no one to tease, no puppet strings to pull."

I smacked him and we both laughed.

"You still owe me a soccer goal contest," I said. "I get to pick the field."

"Right," Mark said, and we knocked fists to seal the deal. "Thanks for coming down."

"Anytime," I said.

"You mean it?"

"Definitely." He'd cut his bangs so both eyes stared back at me, his lips curled up in a nice smile. He definitely wanted to see more of me. Funny, but I wasn't sure if I wanted to see more of him. Or more precisely, *how* I wanted to see him.

Wow. Miracles do happen. Right in the YMCA.

chapter 31

Defrosts and Hot Tamales

If only miracles could happen at the bus stop, too. I stood there Friday morning, wondering how I would look going to the Senior Prom wearing a sandwich board. Why had I come up with this stupid idea anyway? Sure, three of the four had accepted my apology, but the one that mattered most, the one I really wanted to forgive me, hardly even glanced my way.

The kids at the bus stop didn't even blink when I came up — I guess I was looking normal in this thing. I adjusted the straps and bounced from foot to foot to keep warm, waiting for the bus.

"I hear you're having trouble picking out what to wear."

I knew that voice. I'd been longing to hear that voice for weeks.

I sneaked a peek. Jilly wasn't looking at me. She was looking down the street, in the direction the bus came from. I saw her breath curl out of her mouth in the frosty air.

"Pardon me?" I asked politely. Perhaps I had imagined it. Perhaps I wanted so desperately for her to talk to me that I had made up her voice inside my head.

"The all-black underneath is very goth and rather chic, but the sandwich board has got to go," Jilly said, still looking down the street. "It clashes with the ensemble."

"You think so?"

Jilly turned to look at me. "I think you should take it off," she said.

"It's just a suggestion, though. You can decide for yourself what you want to do."

I smiled. "Thanks."

I pulled the sandwich board over my head, setting it up between us. We stood looking at each other, an awkward silence wrapping around us. We'd never had a fight like this before. We weren't sure what to do.

Finally, Jilly took something out of her pocket. "Look how much is left inside." Jilly was holding a half-bitten cherry Tootsie Pop. The entire Tootsie was still there, a round brown dome rising out of the red candy crater.

"How did you do that?" I asked. I'd never seen anyone eat the candy and leave the Tootsie center.

"It wasn't easy," Jilly said, and broke into a grin.

"That's a lot of Tootsie Roll," I said, swallowing hard. Tears stung my eyes and I blinked quickly.

Jilly nodded, still staring at it. "Now what I don't get," she said, "is how long it will last if two people share it."

"There's always another one," I said, pulling two out of my back pocket.

Jilly smiled. "Thanks for what you said in your Intranet letter." She unwrapped one of the Tootsie Pops I handed her and sucked on it. "We do have a lot to talk about."

I took a breath. "When you walked out of my room that night, I went crazy." I spoke softly, as if my words might send her away again. "It was like watching a part of myself walk out. I was so sad and mad I couldn't stand it."

Jilly nodded, taking the Tootsie Pop out of her mouth. "I know what you mean. When I read that last entry you wrote, I went crazy, too. I thought it was the meanest, nastiest, most horrible thing anyone had ever done."

I looked down. "I know," I began. "I'm —"

"You had your turn." She raised her hand to shut me up.

I shut up.

"Some people have teased me about the muzzle and some have felt sorry for me for the things you said on that last page. I kept focusing on that last page, how hateful it was." She paused. "But then I read all the other pages again. And I kept hearing that guy at the bus stop saying that stuff about kissing your pillow and stuff."

She paused and I looked away. It was humiliating to have everyone know I practiced kissing my pillow, even if there were other girls who did the same thing.

"And how much you liked Mark and how you never told me. I can't believe how much you never told me." She stopped talking and blinked rapidly. "But I never really gave you a chance, did I? Never really thought about your life, separate from mine." She sighed. "You were right. I do think about myself a lot."

I didn't know what to say to that, so I didn't say anything.

"You could say 'No, you don't,'" Jilly said, smiling.

"I could," I said. "But —"

"But you won't because you agree with me," Jilly said. "I know."

We stood in silence for a few moments. I shifted my feet and shrugged my shoulders, enjoying how light they felt without the sandwich board. I breathed in the cold January air, letting it fill my lungs as I waited for her to say more.

"If I didn't talk about myself," Jilly asked softly, "who would?"

Her question surprised me. I stepped closer to make sure I heard what she said next.

"Sometimes I feel like no one would care about what I was doing if I didn't talk about it."

I stared at her. "What do you mean?" I said. "I would. I do. I'll talk about you."

"Yeah, but would you say anything good?"

We laughed nervously and then because it was funny.

"You know, Jilly," I said. "Sometimes you do talk too much about yourself. Sometimes it's more about you than it is me. And sometimes I get tired of it. But I never get tired of you. You're my friend. I never tried to tell you what I wanted, so how would you know? Most of the time I didn't know myself."

Jilly nodded. "I know. I just can't get over how dense I was. How I didn't see how you felt about Mark."

I took a deep breath. "Would it have made a difference if I had told you?"

"Honestly, Erin? I don't know. This has really made me think about a lot of things and I don't know what I would have done." She bit her lip. "It's strange to think about because we've never liked the same boy . . ." She paused. "Have we?"

I nodded.

Jilly sighed. "Boy, do we have a lot to talk about." She took off the wrapper from one of the new Tootsie Pops. "And I thought about how I stood in your room and tried to make you pick between two friends." She took another lick. "I shouldn't have done that." She stuck the Pop in her mouth, then pulled it out. "Remember when we hid behind the Martins' house and watched Mr. and Mrs. Martin skinny-dip?"

I looked up. What did that have to do with anything?

"And when you were the only one who would come to my birthday party after I had chicken pox, even though I wasn't contagious anymore?"

I nodded.

"And when you brought me two maps of my classes for Molly Brown Middle School so I wouldn't look like the new girl, even though you had been humiliated by Serena Poopendena?"

I smiled. She'd never used that nickname before.

"Only a real friend would do all that." Jilly looked away, and I knew she had tears in her eyes. But it was kind of hard to tell, since I had them in my eyes, too.

She shook her head. "Okay, enough serious stuff. We need to come up with a signal so when I start talking too much about myself, you give me the signal and I'll know to shut up and focus on someone else for a change."

"A signal? Really?"

"Sure. And check this out." She lifted her pant leg. Not a bruise in sight.

"No more monsters?"

Jilly shook her head. "I put a pillow against the frame." She smiled and jabbed her Tootsie at me. "Put that in your blog."

I laughed. Jilly laughed. We laughed and laughed until we could hardly breathe. As the bus came around the corner, Jilly helped me slide the sandwich board off the sidewalk and behind a bush. I'd deal with it after school.

"What a crazy semester, huh?" Jilly said. "How can so much happen so fast?"

"I don't know," I said. "But I can't believe I got through it." I couldn't help smiling. I had gotten through it. I really had.

"Yes, you did," Jilly said. Her voice held admiration and it made me uncomfortable. I wasn't used to that. "I know you think I'm this really great person and all, Erin, but I'm not. I could never have survived what you did. Never."

We climbed on the bus and found a seat near the front. "First of all, you never would have done the things I did," I told her. "But if you went insane for a day and actually did do them, you would have been fine."

Jilly shook your head. "You've got something that I don't have."

"Stupidity?"

Jilly laughed, then shook her head. "I do stuff because you're there or another one of my friends is there. But you do stuff on your own."

I didn't know what to say to that, so I didn't say anything. I was finding out that silence can be a pretty good thing sometimes. As I settled my backpack at my feet, Jilly got up and sat down in the seat behind me.

"What are you doing?"

"Saving a seat for Rosie," Jilly said.

"Really?"

"Sure," she said. "I want to hear about some of these hot tamales you two talk about."

I smiled and leaned back as the bus lurched forward. A few stops later, Rosie got on and sat with Jilly. As they talked, I glanced out the window, watching the houses and trees pass by, flat clouds streaked above them across the pale blue sky. I felt as if I could slip right through the glass and float up to them, my heart was so light.

I listened to their murmuring behind me, wondering how long it would be before Jilly leaned forward to say something about Bus Boy. My guess was ten Mississippis.

Sighing deeply, I closed my eyes. I didn't know if the three of us could be friends, or how the rest of the year would turn out, but somehow it didn't matter. Whatever happened, things would be okay. *I* would be okay.

"Erin?"

I grinned. Nine Mississippis. I was only off by one.

Monday, June 9

Yes, I'm back to writing in my blog. You didn't think I could stay away forever, did you? But I have taken extra precautions against this disc falling into the wrong hands. I've passworded every file and have signs everywhere to remind me. I'm also going to try not to talk about anyone else but me.

I had a rockin' 13th birthday party in April. It was a big surprise party at the rec center. Jilly and Mom planned the whole thing...I had absolutely NO idea, which, of course, Jilly loved. Everyone was there—even Serena. She gave me a great present, but I didn't know it at 1st. When I opened it I was kind of mad because it was the *Pinocchio* DVD. But when I opened the case, it was the *Erin Brockovich* movie. She'd only put it in the *Pinocchio* cover to freak me out. Mark gave me passes to the Y, Tyler gave me some computer games, and Rosie gave me movie tickets and some tamales — real Mexican ones, not the boys and not the candy. They're awesome. Jilly gave me a necklace and a general gift certificate to the mall...good for any store so I can choose for myself.

I'd like to say the rest of the school year was quiet and good and nothing big happened. But if I did, I'd be lying. I made the MBMS basketball team and tripped over my feet twice going for layups during a playoff game. A picture of me sprawled out on the court facedown made the home page of the Intranet, thanks to Steve who claimed it was only a joke, it wasn't supposed to get published. I asked him why he had taken the picture in the 1st place, but I had to laugh. I did look pretty funny.

I didn't try out for the spring play (there were no vegetables in this 1, but there was something that sounded suspiciously like a piece of fruit), but I did offer to create some computer images that projected on the wall behind the actors during some of the scenes. Unfortunately, there was a bad connection and the circuit blew, and the whole theater went dark right when Jilly was going to do this really important scene. When the lights finally came back on, half the audience was in the bathroom and someone missed their cue, showering the stage with cotton balls B4 the snowstorm was supposed to hit. Jilly handled herself like a pro, saying her lines as if there weren't cotton balls stuck all over her head and several dozen attached to the sequins on the front of her dress.

I asked Tyler to the Spring Dance, but some girl from B Track had already asked him. Not that I *like* like him or anything, but he is kind of cute in a non-geeky, non-nerdy kind of way. Mark had strep and there wasn't anyone else I wanted to go with me (and no 1 asked me), so I helped Jilly get ready to go with Bus Boy.

Just B4 school got out, someone uploaded a picture of Mrs. Porter to the Intranet, but they had doctored it to make it look like she was dancing on a table with 1 of her puppets, a toy whale, on her head.

Steve said it wasn't supposed to go live and that he just wanted to show it to all of us and then get rid of it. He got 1 day of detention and had to write a formal letter of apology to Mrs. AND Mr. Porter (I have a hard time imagining a Mr. Porter. I wonder if he has strings? Oh, wait. That's not nice. Strike that).

So life goes on. 

Things That Are Freaking Me Out 

- Jilly is still going out with Bus Boy. I know his name is Jon Lanner but I will always think of him as Bus Boy. It's been 6 months. This is a world record for her.

- On the 2nd to last day of school, Mark handed me a small pillow, then kissed me. I kissed him back, and we decided we were glad we tried it and we'll never do it again. Mr. Foslowski was right. A good friend can be better than a boyfriend. And I don't have to worry about sweaty hands or bad breath.

- I'm starting to get boobs. Real ones. I had to buy a real bra and get rid of my training bras. Jilly still has the same size trainers. Not that that's important, of course, but I'm just pointing out a fact. I also got a sports bra so I don't bounce when I play basketball or soccer.

Things That Give Me Hope 

- MBMS will continue the Intranet and is also thinking about having a real-live website on the Internet for the school! This will be separate from the Intranet but just as much fun to create. Ms. Moreno has asked me to head up the design if they approve it. We may even start working on it over the summer.

- Serena only sneers half as much as she used to. She actually has a pretty smile.

- Chris is dating this really great girl and I heard that Amanda Worthington is jealous. Can you imagine? What a strange, strange world we live in.

- Mark, Rosie, Tyler, and I are in the same computer camp this summer. I'm psyched!

- And finally, I grew TWO inches this year. That's right, TWO. Maybe the ped really does stop here.

Wow. Would you look at that. I have 5 things that give me hope and only 3 that are freaking me out.

Well, Rosie and I are going to kick the soccer ball around so we can kick some serious butt next week at soccer camp. Tyler's coming along to play goalie.

Contrary to all the laws of seventh grade, it looks like I will move on in the fall.

<u>Click here</u> to find out how I plan to survive eighth grade.

<u>Click here</u> to vote on whether Jilly and BB make it to 7 months.

<u>Click here</u> for a Snickers.

<u>Click here</u>